Invention
of
a
Man

By: Nedra Simone

"Invention of a Man"

Written By
Nedra Simone
"The Play Girl"

www.ThePlayGirl.org

PRINTED IN THE UNITED STATES OF AMERICA

First Edition published 2017

ISBN 9781521453124

Nedra Simone

Dedication

I'm sure if I think long and hard enough I can come up with a million names that I would like to give a shout out to, to say, "YOU" helped make this possible, but then I think...YOU DIDN"T PUT IN ON THIS MAN! So, to keep it simple I will keep it short, intimate and close to home.

I dedicate this book, each piece of creative writing, every product I design and each breath I take to MY greatest creations, "Jasmine Green, J'me Owens and Jaidon Green" (and with the addition of my first grand-monster Jay'Cin Green). She didn't come out of me BUT she seems to always be attached to the hip for some reason.

I would never be able to forget my immediate family. My mother (Vilinda) who has been my ROCK and backbone...my sister (Nicol) who is my ANCHOR and the STRING to my balloon (inside joke) my brother (Jason) who constantly reminds me that I am GREAT and my father (Clarence) who travels the distance to help create my vision. I love you more than words can express. My drive in everything that I do is to ensure financial freedom for my family so that THEY may work to achieve THEIR dreams as well. So...Racine, Little Clarence and Ian you are a part of that goal as well, love you guys.

I also have beautiful children who grew in another person's womb She'mia and Brittany...so proud of you!

Last but not least to someone who I have butted heads with for many years but I know he loves and supports me without a doubt...James, thank you for believing in me when I didn't believe in myself.

I love you guys to life and I will make you proud. I didn't do much at your age but I'm hoping to end "Strong".

CHAPTERS:

Bonus Pages

Chapter One

What I've learned

I know one thing for certain and two things for sure, I have had one very interesting life. Many people will never be blessed enough to have done the things I've done, gone the places I've gone or met the people I've met. But more importantly…many will never know how it feels to be able to say whole-heartedly that "I have a wonderful family". Don't get me wrong, I'm not boasting in any way, I am just stating the facts ma'am. I was lucky enough to have two beautiful, supportive and strong women to kick start my entrance into womanhood. I firmly believe that my grandmother taught us to be "ladies" and my mother taught us to be "women". The "us" that I am referring to is my older sister "Melanie" and since I haven't properly introduced myself as of yet...my name is Erica Brown. Melanie and I have always been told that it is unheard of for sisters to be as close as we are. However, I have to strongly disagree, who else is supposed to know all of your deep dark secrets, other than the person that you created those secrets with; but back to the women that I was initially bragging about. My grandmother was the kind of woman that you never wanted to let down. Hell, the reason I stayed a virgin for as long as I did was because I didn't want to disappoint her. I always felt like she was watching, which sort of puts a damper on hunching and getting pass first base. So a home run was completely out of the question. Her judging eyes burning through my soul like a hot knife through butter was just NOT the kind of foreplay that I was looking for, and trust me when I tell you that says a lot, especially coming from someone who LOVES butter as much as I do. So needless to say when we jumped ship and left town, leaving the guidance of our wonderful grandmother...we lost our ever loving minds. If you were of the male species and you were in our path then you were a prime candidate to be A.T.T.L *(Added to the List).* Don't get me wrong I'm not saying that we were hoes...but we never left home without our "Hoe Bag", which could always be trusted to contain the following items: Change of clothes, toothbrush, hairbrush, extra panties, make-up, lubricant *(LOL)* and condoms. Wait, that list does sound a bit slutty, but what the hell. That was then and this is now. The best we can do now is learn from our mistakes; all 112 of them. That sounds like a brazen number, I know. But just think about where most guys' numbers are before they meet you...while they know you and after they've known you. Shit, I'm a damn virgin! Don't judge me! But back to granny, my grandmother was always there to tell us right from wrong; and notice that I said TELL...and not TEACH; that is because there was no teaching in our household. We lived by the sacred creed *"Do as I SAY, not as I DO"*.

We technically lived two completely separate lives. The main life was led Sunday evening through Friday afternoon just hours after school let out; where our second life was led Friday afternoon through Sunday evening. Of course holiday's, summer breaks and any other day that the Detroit Public School System decided to let us out of the cesspool that they called a learning institution was spent in the comfort and monastery confides of life number two. With each life there were ups and downs. Life number one was fun and adventurous, never knowing what each day would bring. Meaning it was very rare to have everything at once or at least to have everything ON at one time. If we had running water, more than likely we were never in danger of being electrocuted, because the power was more than likely off. I always feel like Chris Tucker when I reminisce about this time in my life.

"Damn Craig, y'all don't never have two things that match, kool-aid, no sugar…peanut butter no jelly…ham no burger…DAAAAMMMMNN"!

But as crazy as it sounds I wouldn't have changed it for the world. Don't misconstrue what I'm saying; I'm sure if my mother could have met and mated with a tennis pro and gave birth to daughters that were intelligent enough to get paid for sleeping around then the world would be "Keeping Up with the Browns" and not the "Kardashians", but that wasn't our fairytale and there are very few knights in shining armor riding around the streets of Detroit. I'm sure there are many that believe they are; but then again we have many colorful characters that dwell the urine stained streets of the "D". Yep, our yellow brick road is just a touch different from the yellow brick road you can find in the wonderful land of OZ. Word of advice...never eat the yellow snow; nine and a half times out of ten it's not lemonade. Where in the hell was I...oh yeah...LIFE "**L**iving **I**sn't **F**or **E**veryone"; and on that note I say "Kill Yourself Detroit". Honestly, the best way to see Detroit is through your rearview mirror. I heard once that they were considering moving all of the humans out of Detroit and turning it into farm land. I only have one question...AND RAISE

DAMN WHAT...murderers, pimps, drug dealers, whores, factory workers and Eminem! Outside of a select few that you can count on one hand with only three fingers left on it, what has Detroit successfully nurtured from that tainted soil that they call a town. This coming from someone born and bred there; and I feel confident in saying that because after almost forty years I have finally come to the realization that "I ain't shit". It's in my blood, my personal make-up. I can't help myself. Some days I honestly think I would have turned out better sliding down my mother's throat or being washed off the sheets with Tide that following Saturday morning, or two Saturday's from then depending on how long it took her to scrap up laundry money. But then again, take a look at the world around us. Maybe Detroit was a great place to be raised. I mean, I really learned how to deal with what this world has thrown at me because of the thick skin that I developed over the years. I mean my skin is so thick that when I die you could probably make a pair of shoes and a handbag out of me. But please make sure that you don't sell me to a pimp and his hoe because the chances of me being bought off the rack only increases my chances of being returned back to my hometown and then it is almost certain that I will NEVER make it out of Detroit...along with everyone else stuck in that God forsaken place. I still don't understand why anyone would intentionally want to stay in Michigan. Every waking minute I would feel like I was stuck in a LIFE SENTENCE! What the hell did I do? Unless they finally make abortions a crime then in that case you might as well place me under the jail and my life sentence I will accept. I would surely rather face life behind the invisible bars of

Seven Mile than to face a mob of angry flying babies when and if I ever make it to Heaven; my little band of Angels. Again, don't judge me this was during a very dark period in my life...puberty!

The difference between now and then is that I now understand that I was completely oblivious to the repercussions of what I was doing during the time that I was mentally absent and unaware that I was creating my very own genocide...and now I realize the magnitude of my sin...and knowing is half the battle. I really need a memory bookmark...oh yeah...grand-ma-ma. I'm not saying that my grandparents were strict but they did live by the rules of yesteryear. My uncle used to tell us about having to go around the corner just to laugh when they were younger. We never really understood it until Melanie and I were sitting down watching a sitcom on television and doing what we believed to be "laughing" when my grandfather said *"sweet if you're gonna laugh...laugh"* and my grandmother co-signed by saying *"yeah, all that giggling is silly"*...WTF! You mean to tell me that there are directions to laughing? So from that point forward or until our grandparents could no longer stand it, we made sure to dig deep and from our loins, bellow out and emphasize both the "H" and "A" as we deliver the most powerful of laughs that we could muster...whenever we felt the urge to laugh. It was either that or just not ever laughing again; which was totally impossible since I personally believe that I am an undercover, under-rated and undiscovered comedian. Honestly speaking, the only thing that I'm missing is the microphone, stage, audience and the courage to stand in front of a room full of sour ass faces waiting on me to personally rewrite their entire day, after coming from their dead end jobs where they secretly wish their stupid bosses were the reason that traffic is at a complete standstill about a mile up. Not to mention their pointless relationships where the last thing that their spouse gave them was a seven day itch and children that they couldn't sell on eBay or the Black Market at a discount. Because let's face it, at best the next generation will be known for bagging single servings of weed and single handedly being the reason that year books will soon be a thing of the past, after they kill each other off while wearing black trench coats; which by the way, now have a bad rep because of these "early ejaculations" that we call children. Okay, where was I? Oh yeah, me and my tangents. If my tomorrow was based on how focused I stayed today, let's just say that tomorrow would more than likely be my last day.

My grandmother, we'll call her "Grandma Lee" was full of advice and fun anecdotes. My aunt used to say that she had the tact of a loaded gun. I never really understood that then, but as time passed and I began to be an able target, that changed. However, I would like to add that she was armed with "Cop Killing Hollow Point Bullets" in that loaded gun of hers. She had a way of building you up and with the force of a body slam by one of the top contenders in the WWF, placing you right back on the mat for an eight count. Grandma Lee would tell you *"that is a beautiful dress, but the way your behind spreads so much it has turned those few flowers into a garden...but it sure is a pretty dress"*, or, *"you got your hair cut, that's cute. I remember when you used to be able to sit on your hair. Do you remember that? It's a shame how you and your sister dogged your hair the way you did. I always said that your hair was your crown and glory. Men don't want a bald headed woman. If that's what they wanted they'd be with another man. But then again, I guess that would explain why neither one of you are married. But it is a cute haircut."* Have I mentioned how much I LOVED this woman? Honestly, I did...well do me a favor and hold that thought. She did however, equip us with the tools to what makes a relationship work and what makes YOU into a person that YOU can stand to look at in the mirror every day. After she would remind us that we *"weren't getting any younger"* she would plant little subliminal relationship clues that have just recently started to bloom. It is only now, thirty something years later that

I have found the urge to water them. Oh Mary, Mary

quite contrary, how does your garden grow? I could

say at this point in time "filled with friggin weeds" but

that will soon change.

My mother has always been the voice of reason and

the ideal role model for keeping your head out of the

clouds and your feet firmly planted on the ground, but

at the same time she supported our dreams. I

sometimes believe that although my sister Melanie

and I both heard the same speeches we each only

took half of what was said. Melanie being the level

headed one and me being the dreamer. I do know

that nothing comes to a dreamer but a dream and

because of that I get my black ass up and make my

dreams reality! I wish I would have realized that

sooner because then maybe I would have been

further in life than I am right now, or that I would

have at least gotten here faster. Not saying that I am
not happy where I am in my life, but I always know
that things could always be better. I am the walking
poster child for *"Talking the talk, but NOT walking the
walk"*. I think this is all because of the creed that was
burned into our minds like a hot prod on a cattle's
rawhide..."*Do as I Say, NOT as I Do*". Which reminds
me; I never told you what I do for a living. I am a
"Relationship EXPERT, Counselor for Confused
Couples, Marriage Mentor" or whatever other fun
phrase you can come up with for being a Life Coach.
That's the title that you receive when you purchased
your certificate off line, gave a few friends some great
advice, caught the bouquet at seven weddings and
helped an old lady across the street. Shit, I sound like
a gosh darn Boy Scout! The kicker is that I am not,
have never been and don't even have the dream of

being married! So again, the poster child for *"Talking the Talk and NOT Walking the Walk"*. How can a person who has never done it before council others on how to keep the fire in a relationship going? Hell, the longest meaningful relationship I had was with a bowl of Lucky Charms the other morning; and I can't even do that right because once all of the marshmallows are gone...so am I. I'm no longer interested in you bowl of cereal and for that reason I must bid you ado. I swear I have the attention span of a damn gold fish. But for some reason, recently things have changed. I saw something last week that flipped a switch in me. But for the life of me I can't remember what it was. It was either two birds in a tree, a cute little old couple walking down the street holding hands or maybe those dogs that were getting it on by the stop sign on my way to the office. But whatever it was…it struck a damn nerve and now *"I think I want a man"*! Because honestly speaking, there is no way that I should be this successful, this beautiful, this creative, this fine…AND THIS DAMN SINGLE! *Where dey do dat at (Ebonics), Ain't nobody got time fa' dat (More Ebonics)*. I woke up this morning with a jolt and have decided that my LIFE starts TODAY!

Who's coming with me?

I have spent a lifetime helping others find and keep love. Maybe I'm so good at it because I know what I am NOT looking for. I think more people would be happy (or happier) if they focused more on what they DON'T want then what they DO want. You could spend the rest of your days trying to find everything that you want in one person, and by the time you realize that they have more qualities that you LOATH

than that you LOVE you've been with the bastard so

long that you're convinced that you need to get a

divorce for a common law marriage. If you decide

early on that you are going to focus on what makes

you unhappy, you'll be happier in the long run and

that way allowing Mr. Wrong in your life would be

close to impossible. Now please don't mistake my

advice with NOT allowing Mr. Wrong into your

BED...because there is nothing like being ravished by a

man who has nothing to do Monday morning. Don't

get it twisted I'm not into rough sex or S&M, but I do

like to know that a man is there. You know, nibble on

my ear...don't Mike Tyson it. Pull my hair, but make

sure you get a full handful you idiot; nothing can ruin

the mood like you pulling one lonesome strand of hair

and pissing me all the way off. I don't mind you

ripping my blouse, dress or panties...just as long as you're able to replace it, preferably with something nicer. Shit if you can't even afford to take a bitch on a "*Rainbow*" shopping spree...then best believe you will not be getting to the pot of gold at the end of my rainbow! I think sex is just that SEX and you can have that with just about anyone. I do try to, as the younger kids say it "*stay in my lane*", my age lane that is. Although I have to admit that I did veer off the beaten path and allowed a youngster to sip on my honey pots sweet nectar and although the sex was intense and at sometimes mind blowing, when the young buck went into a naked version of "So You Think You can Dance" by doing the "Dougie"; I knew then that it might be a good idea to keep my Venus "Guy" Trap from off the playground or at least put a parental warning on it. So, no more kids for the kid, I have learned my lesson. My mind is screaming at the top of MY lungs *"get your lazy ass up"*, but my body is just NOT trying to hear that right now. Again, a broken relationship due to lack of communication; mind and body should work together as one. Hell, how else am I supposed to *"cum"* so I can get off and get on with the rest of my day? If you didn't get it, I am masturbating; yep, you heard me right. I am double clicking my mouse, getting to know myself a little better; rocking my own world...you get the picture. Needless to say I am NO master at masturbating. Being a control freak is no picnic. I can't even let go of the reigns for one second to get myself off. I would be a much happier person if I could make it to the finish line every once in a while. I believe that is the reason that I am not a fan of oral sex. It makes me feel vulnerable and I HATE that feeling. Why can't orgasms be like work? I get "off" at five...why can't I "get off" (*if you know what I mean*) at the same time each day? I would be nicer to people, my skin would be clearer; I would genuinely all around be a better person. My staff would definitely like me more. When I tell you that they probably HATE me sometimes...most of the time...freak it...all of the damn time! But who cares "*who gon check me boo*"! No really, I pay them well enough to where they can deal with whatever I pitch their way. So with a new focus on life...almost reaching my peak...and hitting my snooze button now eleven times...I am ready to start this day.

****

One long, hot shower later and a second attempt at NOT "cumin" I now must decide what sexy armor I will bless this mundane world with this fine morning. I hear my custom California King calling me faintly in the distance "Erica Brown, Erica Brown come lay your fine brown ass back down". As tempted as I am to jump back in the comforts of my cozy best friend I know that I must rebuff his advances and move forward with my plans of conquering this world, one relationship at a time. This morning I have an appointment with an older woman and her young boy toy to assist them with rekindling the fire in their marriage. The wife said that for some reason her young husband just can't get it up anymore. They have tried the doctors and even the doctors stated that he is a perfect bill of health. I personally can already tell her that her husband is fine and so is his flame...it's just not burning for her. With that said I believe that I will wear this new soft pink, back out cashmere dress that I recently purchased off line through some clothing company in China. Coming right above the knee and swooping sensually just above the curve of my lower back to reveal a naughty little tattoo that I got when I was in my early twenties. The tattoo says "Caught You Looking". I make it my business to place my tattoos in areas that if you don't "know me...know me"; then you have no idea about my body ink. Covering your body with all sorts of graphic ideas illustrating who you thought you WERE and how you FELT at a certain time in your life is not necessarily MY forte; but to each his own. I just personally feel that if I place someone's name on my body that name better last as long as that tattoo. I am not your personal billboard. I can understand for sentimental reasons to commemorate someone's life or death...but if you haven't died then I would only feel obligated to kill you...jk...or am I? I better not kid like that especially with my murderous background.

Invention of a Man

I have decided on these rhinestone stilettoes that I had made by one of my personal stylist. My stylist "Sincerely" creates and delivers a new pair of shoes every two weeks. Who knew that a young man from the Bronx could be so crafty and intuitive when it comes to women's clothing and accessories? His mother did...that's who knew. When a young boy struts around in his mother's high heels with a face full of make-up begging for the newest Barbie...best believe that nine and a half times out of ten he's going to end up playing with KEN when he gets older...I'm just saying! And before you start hating me I only said nine and a half times out of ten so that leaves some wiggle room for the guys that actually still prefer the vagina. At times I have to say I sort of understand the choice to cross over when it comes to men...because I

KNOW how good dick is. I honestly don't have a personal problem with same sex relationships. I would rather a person live happily with someone of the same sex before they live miserably and mistreated by someone of the opposite sex. The only problem that I have ever had with those who live a homosexual lifestyle is that with WOMEN (*who act like men*) why do you feel the need to cut all of your hair off and wear five sport bras to smash your breast in. Who wants to have a 24/7 mammogram? For WOMEN (*who like butch women*) doesn't being a lesbian mean that you enjoy the look of another beautiful woman? Isn't it hypocritical to find a woman who looks like a man? I thought that's what you were trying to get away from. For MEN (*who THINK they are acting like wom*en) who in the hell are you imitating? I have NEVER acted the way you act not one day in my life outside of when I am imitating YOU! I'm all for expressing yourself and living the way you want (*as long as it doesn't hurt anyone else*)...but who in the hell stays stuck during the halftime of a high school football game? Because let's face it, you are mimicking a damn majorette! Hey ref...call the game back in already. And finally MEN (*who are living down low*) you have to be the greediest people I know. You want your hot dog and you want your cake! How dare you creep through society lines just to escape the label of being GAY! Well; "I ain't scared of you mutha@#!%*. I will call a spade a spade and **F**ish **A**nd **G**rits is exactly that! I think it is right selfish to hand me some damn e-coli and salmonella poison that I didn't even ask for. Pick one side of that fence and stay your ass there; although I understand that you most enjoy perching atop of the erect spikes of that picket fence...**BUT BE A MAN AND TELL THE WORLD THAT YOU LOVE DICK**! I will support anyone who has the courage to stand up for themselves and what they believe in. Do you...don't talk about it, be about it!

As I look in the mirror I am beyond pleased with the beautiful specimen of divine decadence staring back at me. If I was you I'd fuck me...oh, wait I already did that. I digress then. The new hair color that I reluctantly tried is actually starting to grow on me. I've never really been into changing the color of my hair drastically, I am a more subtle soul and I am more inclined to going with a style that you really have to stare at to even realize that something is in fact "different" with my hair. So yes, my dear "Watson" I did do something different with my hair. Nonetheless, I am still shocked at the new coif direction that I allowed my stylist to take me in. After years of restoring my hair back to the natural state that my mother, father, grandparents, GOD and Native American ancestry first blessed me with; I have opted to keep my locks as dark as humanly possible. This is with the assistance of "Cream of Nature" and the sweet little lady who thinks that because my hair fairs past the middle of my back that I am naturally coming in for my monthly dose of Virgin Remy hair. Whenever she sees me she tries to push this darn borrowed hair on me. *"You look good with 1B Miss Brown, that good look for you. That's you color"*. Why does every black woman with any sort of length or shine to her hair have to be wearing weave? I hate when people make assumptions. Like the little lady that has been doing my eyebrows for the past seven years. Each time I go in the salon it never fails that she asks me after she rips my eyebrows out of my face..."*You want lip*". And each time it irritates me beyond belief. One day she is going to catch me on a bad trip and I'm going to reply back "You want me to punch you in your lip"? Anyway, back to my new hairstyle; now I have two silver/white/grey streaks. One on each side of my head. My stylist stole the look from the lady on that television show "What NOT to wear". So far I have had to fight men off with a stick (*but that is an average Monday for me*). I guess the difference now is that I have broadened my field of pickings. I often look in the mirror and wonder who this cougar is gazing back at me. That gray is fierce!

My staff always tells me that I am overdressed for work or the age old *"are you going somewhere after you leave here"*? Why must we dress for Monday?

Invention of a Man

Why can't we make Monday dress for us? I am the captain of my own destiny and I make fashion decisions that I feel will upgrade my life and my lifestyle. I am a firm believer in always being ready because you NEVER know who you're going to meet. I used to hold a position helping displaced women and children with an apartment community who set aside so many units to help the less fortunate. Hold your applause because it was all money driven. Atlanta Housing paid top dollar to house these people, the company I worked for could give two shits about them. My job was to assist these ladies to get back on their feet. After a few weeks on the program I could no longer stand it. It made my skin crawl to see these women walk into my office day in and day out at all times of the day in their pajamas, head rags and house shoes. What in the hell if opportunity knocked?

What would you do then? You aren't even ready. I decided to help give the ladies an overhaul. How can you really expect a person to strike out and do better if they didn't even know better? How do you convince someone that there is a wonderful world out there just waiting for them, if the only happily ever after they have ever experienced has been at the end of a storybook or Disney movie? People who have been beaten down by life have lost their drive to dream big and without giving them a taste of the greatness that is out there they will never really know what they want. It's a proven fact that people who don't know better will more than likely not do better. Test the theory and see for yourself.

Anyway, I decorated the office to where when you walked through the main door you were forced to read (*if they could read*) framed quotes asking them questions about if they were ready for what comes

next...

- DID YOU BRUSH YOUR TEETH; WASH YOUR

  FACE AND SHOWER TODAY?

- ARE YOU PREPARED IF SOMEONE WAS HERE

  TO HIRE YOU?

- WOULD YOU BE READY FOR YOUR PRINCE

  CHARMING?

When you reached the end of the hall and each

framed question & quote you ran face to face with the

real YOU in a full length mirror that stood at attention

outside of my office door. If you were NOT ready, then

I would NOT be ready to assist you with even the

simplest request. It was as simple as that. My goal was

to throw an event that these ladies would remember

for the rest of their lives and being that most of these

women came from shelters or off the cold streets of

Atlanta, I had to initiate a "Black Dress Drive" just so they could have something to wear for the evening. I had black dresses coming in from everywhere in every style and size. From simple to sexy to mourning to mayhem we had dresses for days. On the day before the event I recruited a styling team that shut down their shop to exclusively pamper these ladies free of charge. They were fried, dyed and laid to the side by the time we came from out of there.

The evening of the secret event there was a buzz that swarmed through the streets because no one knew what I had up my sleeves and it made for an even stronger panic due to the fact that I didn't have on any sleeves...so with that said anything was liable to happen. At five thirty by invitation only, I requested that the women be showered, shaven and dressed to impress (*as best they could*) and standing in the parking lot in front of the apartment turned project manager office where we would hold our weekly meetings. The cool crisp air on that April 24th was paired with a comfortable breeze that swirled around the waves of anticipation. Others who were not in this program gawked in the distance, necks stretched to their maxed length, some necks even turning corners.

My mother had a name for those kind of people..."Rubber Necker's", which by the way are the leading cause for making traffic back up after an accident. They'll look but they won't help!

Anyway, where was I...oh yeah, "It was a calm cool April evening and all through the hood. Packs of hood rats were peeping to see what was good". No really, thirty ladies stood in elegant new attire, actually make that twenty-eight stood and two sat due to the fact they were both one leg amputees. Even they rolled up looking like new money with their new looks. Their wardrobe actually worked out perfectly. Not too often do you find a left and right amputee with the same shoe size. The night couldn't have been more perfect.

In the distance you could see the headlights from a line of luxury coaches pulling in to take my "Cinderella's for a Day" off to their ball. From the bulging of their eyes it was quite apparent that many, if not all of these ladies had never had the pleasure of riding in a limousine. Honestly I could have stopped at the dresses, hair and make-up and they would have been more than thankful...but that's just not my style. I believe that everyone should feel special if for just one day...which oddly enough was the title of the evening; "If Only for One Night". There is something about "not knowing" that gets the senses to racing. So when five stretch limousines pulled up in the ghetto

that April night the rumor mill began to spin. As the

ladies loaded into the fine automobiles to be whisked

away to places unknown, palms were sweaty and

newly arched eyebrows that were once neatly placed

in the center of foreheads now sat dangerously close

to hairlines as anticipation reached its peak as we

pulled up to a beautiful home that you would not be

surprised to see in the pages of "Better Homes &

Gardens". Although the sun had since fallen leaving

only traces of an illustrious orange and pink hue over

the sky, you could still see the fine details of this

Spanish style home with stucco siding and large

curved orange pottery style shingles. The landscaping

boast bountiful fruit trees and lavish hills of rolling

green lawn all held in by what seemed like a

continuous garden of colorful flowers of all types that separated the lawn from the actual pavement.

As if what nature had masterfully and artistically laid out before you was not enough, I had personally handpicked and hired thirty of the most handsome and sexy gentlemen that my favors could call in. Perched at attention they stood with the force that not even a tornado could move. In their black tuxedoes, bow ties, military shined shoes and holding a single red long stemmed rose. My line of clean cut prime choice men were there to show how a man was supposed to treat a lady. Their mission was simple...make this night unforgettable; and that is exactly what they did. Every lady has a little princess in them, sometimes she gets lost in the haze of kissing so many frogs. The evening was lovely, catered food, a beautiful setting, stylish chariots and memorable times…"If Only for One Night". As the evening slowly vanished as the second hand of the clock counted down the close of this fantastic night.

Ten…Nine…Eight…Seven…

The ladies had danced, laughed, been served and pampered by some of Atlanta's hottest men. They were allowed to walk a mile in MY shoes to see how the other side lives, hopefully urging and provoking them to seek out and obtain the means to make this an everyday reality for them.

Six…Five…Four…Three…

For most of our "Bells of the Ball" they exited the mansion with their shoes in their hands as appose to on their feet (*or foot*) and their heads in the clouds. Which was fine for the moment because it was just THAT…their moment.

Two…One…

Back to reality was the verbal declare as we pulled back into the dreary dwellings of their everyday mundane lives. I was only obligated and contracted to spend four hours a day, five days a week with these ladies and I couldn't even help feeling sorry for myself so I could imagine what they felt being the possessor of a key to these crumbling brick palaces. No, honestly I couldn't even visualize being here. So allow me to retract my last statement, I could not imagine what these women felt day in and day out. When I first started this project my biggest concern was that the tires on my 2012 black on black Range Rover Sport would probably catch some sort of a disease rolling across the streets of this slum. You must understand that just because I was born and raised in Detroit it doesn't mean that I lived in the ghetto. Besides it wasn't even until after we moved to Atlanta that we

lived in an apartment. It blew my mind to know that I

was sharing an entire WALL with a complete stranger;

two totally different lives being lived on each side of

this connecting wall that we shared. I am sure that my

life at the time was far less interesting to them, so my

pleasure was listening ear to glass, glass to wall to the

heated episodes of the couple next door. If only I had

a remote to change it from Spanish to English or at

least turn on the darn subtitles. I could have actually

solved all of my problems had I just paid attention in

Spanish class so I could at least have an outline of

what's going on...hell I'm creative, I could just make

up the rest.

The initial joy that overwhelmed me that previous

evening was somehow overshadowed by the feeling

of defeat the next day when those same smiles came

tumbling down as the ladies approached me wanting to receive the telephone numbers of their suitors. Although obvious to me that the gentlemen from last night were just there to fill a void as a favor, it was heartbreaking to them to inform them in the best way I knew how…"That's was just for THAT night". I guess I didn't think that far into this plan of mine; so to avoid being looked upon to fix an unfixable situation that would require me actually being a "Fairy God Mother", I leaped at the chance to jump ship when another property opened. I've notice that I did a lot of "ship jumping" in my earlier days; crazy thing to do for a person who can't swim. Hell, life is all about sinking or swimming…or floating which is another thing that I learned growing up.

Sink...Swim or Float! Between my grandmother and mother I was taught four things that I would not understand until I was "of age" and that was this:

1) Stop wasting your time looking for the perfect man (*might be woman in your case*). There is no such thing. You will miss everything life has to offer standing around waiting and looking.

2) A man (*might be woman in your case*) is only as faithful as his (*her*) options. If you place your man in a room with no people, windows or doors you have a good man on your hands.

3) If you get the opportunity, marry your best friend. I am not referring to your childhood best friend...but your final best friend (*I will explain more later on*).

4) And finally…people will tell you who they really

   are and what they want; YOU just have to

   listen.

My grandmother would ask me all the

time…"What's Your Story"…well just sit back and

listen because I'm about to tell you!

Dear Reader

Let's play a **MEMORY** game...

First person you KISSED _____

Last person you KISSED _____

Who took your VIRGINITY _____

Last person you COPULATED with _____

Favorite Position _____

Are you PASSIVE or AGGRESSIVE _____

Are you HORNY right now _____

First person you fell in LOVE with _____

Person you regret the MOST _____

Person you regret the LEAST _____

Your GO TO for a BOOTY CALL _____

If you could have one more night with ONE
person from your past who would it be and why

_____

_____

_____

What kind of lover do you consider yourself and
Why

_____

_____

_____

Chapter Two

On the Prowl

I am looking at this person standing in front of me and if looks could kill she would be dead in about three seconds. I am envisioning a baby grand piano falling on top of this lady or one of those ACME weights that used to crush the ever determined Wiley Coyote back in the day as she slowly tells the Starbucks barista what she wants. "And please make sure that you don't add as much foam as you did last time, I had more foam than anything. Also be sure to slide the sleeve all the way up, I nearly burned my hand when I was here a few weeks ago". Bitch if you don't take that cup of pasteurized foam and move your receding hairline to the side I am going to drown you in that double mocha, foam Grande with breast milk in it! I seriously need to get my coffee before I do something...that would "although please the hell out of me"...I'm sure someone will find regret in one day. When I FINALLY get to the counter I damn near forget what I even want. The pretty strawberry blonde taking my order is looking at me smiling but you already know that she is saying under her breath "please don't let this one be like the last one". I, without being asked any questions blurt out "don't worry this order will be painless". She bats what I believe to be her own beautiful long eyelashes (*I hate her now*) as she innocently says "I'm sorry ma'am, what did you say". I reply with an unemotional "don't worry about it; may I have a "Cocoa-Coffee" and two chocolate chip cookies". As she nods her head and begins to prepare my order I spy with my beautiful slanted green eyes what has to be the mold for what God himself used to create Adonis. Although he is sitting down I can tell just by looking at him that he has to stand at a mouthwatering six foot three inches; which prayerfully means that he hangs at the very least a relaxed eight inches...but you know what sort of cruel jokes God can play. I have met men who look like they should be changing light bulbs for a living or some other tall job like apple picking, rescuing kittens from trees or a top shelf getter and when it gets down to the nitty-gritty he looks like he should be in "Stage One Pampers". So, if you were under the impression that BIG meant BETTER, I hate to be the bearer of bad news but...you might be sadly mistaken. Within seconds, I have discovered what appears to be the latest Michael Kors watch that retails for a minimum of $3,800.00 (*impressive*), meticulously polished Prada shoes (*$1,750.00*) and an Italian cut suit (*$5,200.00*) that fits as perfectly as a second skin...which by the way is a dark (*no sugar/no cream*) coffee brown. His dark skin melts seamlessly with his almost black soul piercing eyes.

I want to tell this cheerleader behind the counter to hurry the hell up and while she's at it place the warm cookies back on the rack because I think I have found just the thing to satisfy my sweet tooth. As if my stare wasn't obvious enough when he looked up and in my direction I added a playful wink for good measure. I hold my breath to see if my advances will be accepted or declined. As I had suspected he reveals the most perfect set of pearly whites that I had ever seen and casually nods letting me know that I had his permission to move on to second base.

It takes me a second to locate my wallet so that I can

retrieve my card and it just now dawned on me that I

changed purses this morning. I clearly must have left

my ENTIRE wallet in my other Coach bag...SHIT...keep

cool Erica. This is so NOT ME...but hell, every girl is

entitled to at least ONE off day; and this is mine. I

remove my "iPhone 7", Mac Glass Lip Gloss and

business card case to get to my *"In Case of Emergency*

Stash" and place them on the counter. I've made it a

habit to always hide at least a twenty in each purse

for cases like this. I hand the cheerleader behind the

counter the crisp twenty dollar bill, grab my change,

utter a quick "Thanks", flip my hair and fall into my

most severe "Samantha Jones" strut...I am forced to

halt my efforts for what could possibly turn into a

wonderful afternoon delight when I see the manager

approach my future sex slave and hands him what

appears to be an application...FOR EMPLOYMENT!

Well I'll just be damned, are you serious? I have to

hurry and get this cup of Joe in me because my radar

is all off this morning. I try my best to slide past this

guy like a ghost but that animal attraction that I exude

is no match for these mere mortals; now I have to be

creative in diffusing this situation that I have created. I

am almost out of the door and just about to kick it

into second gear when a strong hand grabs mine.

With a slight jerk I spin around on the balls of my feet

to stand face to chest (*humph...help me baby Jesus*)

with my prey. For once in my life I am at a loss for

words so he decides to take the lead. "Good morning

beautiful, how are you fairing this fine day? I was

hoping to sit down with you to finish the conversation

that we had already started with our eyes". I hear his

sultry voice but can't seem to get that darn

application out of my head. I reply quickly with an obvious flirtatious remark *(I can't seem to shut this damn thing off)*. "Our eyes...maybe you misunderstood my morning glare, my apologies". "Are you certain, because by the look in your eyes I was almost positive that you had already gotten down to the undies?" He stands towering over me with the aroma of what appears to be my favorite men's cologne. "Boxers" he said flashing those pearly whites again. I quickly wondered if they were veneers. I've learned that men are just as fake as women these days...if not more. "Excuse me" I said, knowing that I had been caught. "I'm wearing boxers" he said. My mind totally went left as I pictured myself in those boxers and him lying naked on my California King. It was close to impossible to hide the smirk on my face emphasized by my rosy cheeks as my body temperature rose to a dangerous degree. I was certain

that you could have fried an egg on my ample ass.

Maybe we would try that out one of these weekends.

WTF was I doing...this man probably has knock off

everything...as he stands there holding a damn

employment application. I am beaming inside to know

that my decision last year to have corrective Lasik

surgery paid off. I see you Mr. UNEMPLOYED and I

don't need any more PROJECTS. My plate is full and

the only thing you can bring to the table is your

appetite. As the saying goes..."I know what I bring to

the table and I have NO PROBLEM eating

alone...AMEN! The sweet smell of "Givenchy"

embodies me and it takes a second to break free. "I'm

sure that line works on girls with one name,

however"...he interrupts me swiftly "Speaking of

names, you never gave me yours. My name is Edward

Sparks". You would think with a name that powerful he would be on a different playing field. How I would LOVE to be his private cheerleader. "I'm not in the giving spirit this morning Mr. Sparks. Perhaps you should wait for the next pretty lady to waltz on past you, maybe she'll be more your speed". I politely retrieve the hand that he had held captive during this entire exchange of morning pleasantries. As I turned away from him, being sure to over exaggerate every move; his words followed me nearly knocking me to my knees. "Who ever said that you were pretty?" I spun around fast enough to be mistaken for a spinning top. Who knew that blood could boil so fast? "I beg your pardon" were the only words that I managed to muster. I'm not saying that every man in this world is supposed to find me desirable...however, THIS damn man should. Has he lost his ever loving mind? Hell, I'm the Beyoncé' to his Jay Z...the Kim to his Kanye...the Oprah to his Stedman, honey you better recognize greatness when you see it! Before the steam began to escape from out of my little teapot, he came back with, "I was just saying that pretty is the understatement of the century. I would feel more confident using REGAL or ANGELIC".

I don't often find myself at a loss for words but right now Mr. I-NEED-A-JOB had me wanting to be the SUGAR to his MAMA. Before I could utter a word he approached me and reached down with the grace of a peacock and I swear it felt like time had stood still. When he slowly rose I noticed that he had detached an unsightly napkin that had attached itself to my beautiful shoes. I felt perplexed. He had done it again, made me feel as if "he" was the catch of the day and I was the "appetizer". It almost reminded me of the time when my sister Melanie was enrolling in college; back when Morris Brown actually stood for something. As she stood in line with an arm full of paperwork, wearing a short blue and white polka-dot summer dress showing off legs that would make "Tina Turner" sit her ass down somewhere. Two guys; that she believed were trying to "holla" at her through the office window, had been trying to get her attention for about five minutes. As she strutted past them with the grace of a cheetah and walked over to the parking space that had once occupied her baby daddy's late model "Cadillac" she noticed a pile of glass from what was once the passenger window. In shock she spun around to see those same two young men shaking their head. "We were trying to tell you that somebody was stealing your shit shawty". Defeated and

embarrassed is what she felt as she walked home
afraid to tell her baby daddy that her "assumption and
conceit" was the reason that Marta would be "**M**oving
(*these two*) **A**fricans **R**apidly **T**hrough **A**tlanta". You
would be safe to say that she spoke to EVERY person
that approached her after that; which might be the
reason that her list of knuckleheads is a mile long...a
Georgia mile (*which is never really a mile*).

I can't help but to hide my face as shame covered it
like a blanket. How is it that I am letting a man who is
obviously beneath me and under my pay scale make
me feel inferior? I politely thank him and get to high
stepping. I bet my damn cocoa-coffee is cold now! As I
walk away I can hear him as clearly as if he was still
standing right next to me; "Hopefully our paths will
cross again". I don't know how likely that is, hell, I
didn't have any plans on visiting the unemployment

office any time soon. But I will admit that he might just turn into my favorite barista now. Out my peripheral I believe that I see the "Coffee Cheerleader" dash out the door yelling something but I can't quite hear her over the roar of city traffic. Atlanta traffic is always a pain in the ass. Whatever it is, I'm sure it's not important...I got my change.

****

As I walk into my office the first thing I notice is the clock on the wall and either I'm late or it needs a battery. My cute as a button receptionist scurries over to me with the excitement of a grade school child on Christmas morning who realizes that Santa Clause must have misplaced his NAUGHTY list, because she ACTUALLY got presents this year. I swear she reminds me of myself a million years ago. "Ms. Brown, you must have a four leaf clover under your pillow" she says as she smirks exposing the cutest dimple in the world. I mean I have dimples too...just not on my face. "What on earth are you talking about Ashlyn"? She's right on my heels as I enter my office and hang my scarf on my vintage coat tree, a super find that I ran across while doing my monthly antique store shopping spree. It's unique because it actually looks like a tree. Made from branches with the tips being dipped in 24 carat gold. It has hidden stones throughout and a glitter in its hue. It was one of my best finds to date. My scarf complimented the tree almost as if they were made for each other. The weather was so nice that I didn't need a coat; just a simple cover up did just fine. "Did you forget that time went up last night"? As soon as she uttered the words I remembered, which now meant that I was almost an hour late for my ten o'clock meeting. My mind is all over the place, even with the delightful smell of chocolate and strawberry croissants roaming the halls of the agency, I still can't manage to shake the aroma of "Mr. Can't Clock In". I have to pull myself together. I feel agitated and disheveled, it's almost like I've forgotten something. I hate that feeling. The same feeling of NOT being in control...takes me back to my "peaking problem". My very own personal "Dear Watson" hands me a list of what I need to do, some papers that need my John Handcock on them and my coffee that she rescued from my arms when I first walked in today. Just as I suspected...my damn coffee is cold. Apparently Ashlyn has been talking a mile a minute but I can't recall a single word. I catch her at the end of her soliloquy. "That's why I asked if you had a four leaf clover under your pillow" she says as she stands smiling with teeth that prove we have a

GREAT dental plan! My bewildered look suggests that I didn't hear anything that she said. "Woman you would be headless without me. Your ten o'clock called to push back to noon which means that luckily you have an open one hour slot available". Finally I compute what she has said and snap back to reality. "Sweetie let me hit you with the headline...It has NOTHING to do with luck...what you're looking at is SKILL! Now watch me work"! I return my attention back to the heap of files on my desk to find today's session. "I simply adore you Erica, I have so much to learn; and that dress is killing them today. I don't know how you manage to make it down the street without being mauled". If she was anyone else I would tell her to pull back on the reigns because they were doing too much...or THE MOST as the young people say nowadays. However, I know that she means every word. I told you that she is my clone. I simply say to her "People attract what they exude. Animals maul and bite things. I'm a lady, so only the finest in all accounts must apply". She smiles before she exits and closes the door behind her. Not that I need to stretch my legs or anything but at that moment I decide to walk over to my floor to ceiling windows that overlook the city. I'm supposed to be reading over this file in my hands so that I will be ready when my (*now*) twelve o'clock appointment arrives. For some reason my mind is still wandering and I travel back to what I just told Ashlyn; if a person attracts what they exude then why did "Mr. Are Y'all Hiring" even approach me? What the hell am I exuding? I walk over to my floor length mirror just to see if I was presenting the image of "NOW HIRING". No, I didn't. What was it about him that made me keep thinking about him?

This is not me, I don't dwell on people who serve me no purpose...and he was not even in my league. Also, this stinging feeling of me forgetting something has left me very uneasy. Did I leave the iron on? No, you don't iron cashmere (*fool*). Did I leave the oven on? No, I don't even go in my kitchen, that's what I have a chef for (*crazy*). WHAT IS IT DAMN IT? My thoughts are interrupted as Ashlyn knocks and enters. "Yes, Ash, what is it" I said as I turned to face her? Did you not hear the intercom; I said that your twelve o'clock was here" she whispered as if they were standing right behind her. "Are you okay Erica"? "I'm fine, please see them in" I replied. Where had the time gone, it was just eleven. Had I been standing here daydreaming all this time? Something's definitely wrong...but what is it?

Following behind Ashlyn is a fairly attractive woman in her mid to late sixties and trailing behind her is a casually dressed man (*boy*) of Italian decent. The older woman, who after glancing again at their file is the widow of an oil tycoon, her name is "Valerie Glover". She is immaculately dressed in a blended silk suit, pencil skirt with a matching blazer. The broach attached to the lapel already told me that she could buy and sell me ten times over. Her shoes, although not high enough for my taste exhibited little to no wear at all and I'm sure she didn't buy them just for this meeting, which means that her "show closet" is probably to die for. Every strand of hair was in place and was a beautiful salt and pepper mix. Not the staged coif of color like I had...but she was doing it. I would feel confident saying that she would have no problem getting any man her own age. However, the way that she carried herself told me that she didn't feel like being bothered with a man that life had already trained up and molded. She was looking for something that she could mold and manage herself. She just hadn't mastered the art of training a man up the way you want them; I could help her with that. He walked with a cocky strut that said he knew exactly what SHE was doing and that HE would play along as long as HE got what he wanted. Dressed in dark indigo blue relaxed jeans, a button up Ralph Lauren long sleeve peach shirt and a tan colored blazer with darker colored brown elbow patches...he looked like the perfect "boy toy". They both shook my hand and took a seat on the turquoise modern sofa sitting beneath a beautiful oil "finger painting" that was created by the talented little children at the "Wade Walker YMCA" in Stone Mountain, GA. Their art teacher Mr. Ali Lowery **@b3autiful_s0ulz** was acting director at that time and brought so much life to that program, all I added was money, huge difference. Not everything in life cost a million dollars...some things are just WORTH a million dollars. This piece was a "thank you" for the generous donation that I made a few years ago to their arts department.

"Thank you for seeing us today and please accept my apology for being tardy. I am so glad that you could squeeze us in. As you know, my name is Valerie Glover and this is Neal" she smiled softly as she made the formal introductions. "The pleasure is all mine Mrs. Glover" I say as I so eloquently ignore the hungry glare of her husband. As I stated earlier, there is NOTHING wrong with her husband's flame...trust me!

I opened their file (*the file that I had already supposedly studied*). "What brings you to my office today"? I say as I smile and cross one silky leg over the other. I will do this at least one hundred more times to ensure that I keep her male counterparts attention. Not in a vulgar way, but the equivalent of a nudge that your grandmother would give you if you started dozing off in church. "Well, there seems to be a void that's growing between us and I want to try to correct the problem before it becomes too large for us to get over". The look on her face showed distress and embarrassment...I felt sorry for her. Before I could interject Neal began to speak. "There really isn't a problem or "void" as she stated. I've told her several times that I love her and nothing has changed. I can't correct her own insecurities". I glanced at her to see if she was buying it...she wasn't, apparently she had "been there, done that". "Well Neal that's where I'm going to assist you. I am a touch unethical when it comes to my particular approach, but it gets the job

done". I smiled at them both before I continued.

"Today's visit is just our initial meeting, our "Meet and

Greet" so to say. Each week you will be given a

different homework assignment that I expect both of

you to do. But before we start I need to ask some

questions". I stand up and walk around to my desk

retrieving two identical silver folders. I hand each of

them a folder and begin my normal

"Relationship Start-over Speech".

Like to hear it...here it go!

"Anyone who ever said that a relationship is NOT hard

work...must have never been in one. The trick to

making your relationship work is simple; BOTH parties

MUST give no less than 100%. The days of 50/50 are

gone...or dead in the water as the young folks say. The

saying that "there are plenty of fish in the sea" is VERY

true and accurate. However, if you aren't a good fisherman you'll catch more that you'll need to throw back OR you'll catch more than you ever bargained for. Too often we become comfortable and complacent after we've caught the one we want to be with. Yes, the person you love should love you unconditionally, through it all, and for better or worse...but let's be honest; who wants to look at the same "relaxed person day in and day out? The only time looks are NOT important is when your partner is BLIND"! Neal mumbled a very discreet "Amen" and in return I continued this time shooting for him. "Now, there are times and situations where relationships are built on an "understanding and/or arrangement". Or let's call it what it is...a financial kind of love. But let me tell you a little about those types of relationships...often times, the one holding the bank is the one who sets the rules and quite frankly there are way more players out there ready to take that persons spot". I was thrown off when Mrs. Glover shot back with a perfectly timed "Amen" of her own. Clearly I have gotten their undivided attention. Now all I need to do is implement some couples activities and one of three things will follow: they will live happily ever after...one will move on to something better...or they BOTH will understand and accept a new set of rules and respect the PLAYER and the GAME!

Before they go I hand them something that I developed called "You've Got Love". You've Got Love is a relationship kit designed to assist in all levels of relationships. It is not just a product but a service. A service that if used and followed correctly will replace any products and/or ideas from yesteryear about how to reignite the flame in your relationship. I hand

Invention of a Man

Valerie the kit along with the instructions and I bid them both farewell and walk back around to my desk. Once I sit down I quickly realize that my cellphone *(or cellular device as my father always says)* was not on my desk where it always is. I rise from my desk and walk over to my coat tree where I sometimes hang my purse...not there. I next go over to the stylish armoire turned file cabinet to see if I had mistakenly laid it there while retrieving the files...but the files were already lying on my desk when I entered. Just where in Sam hell is my phone? Not that I was waiting for a phone call or was in dire straits to make a call BUT it's my damn phone and I want to use it when I want to use it. I head out to my reception area where everyone is looking at me like I have mud on my face or something. I guess I should come out of my coffin more often.

I approach the elegantly designed reception desk and waiting area where Ashlyn is sitting pretending to work…when I know that she is probably on Facebook or Instagram. "Ash, when you took my coffee out my hand this morning, did you happen to take my purse too"? "I didn't take it, you hung it up on the coat tree by the door" she says helpfully but ever so nonchalantly. "That's what I thought, thanks" I begin to walk away but turned back around. "Ashlyn, I think what I'm really trying to say is, have you seen my cell phone"? "Oh, well in that case, no, sorry I haven't seen it. When was the last time you used it? Because I know that I had called you about ten times before you walked in". She looked about as confused as I felt. I turned away mechanically as I began to retrace my footsteps for the morning.

- Woke up (*like dis*)

- Double clicked the mouse

- Took a shower

- Double clicked the mouse

- Washed my hands

- Did my hair

- Picked out my suit of armor

- Got dressed

- Grabbed my breakfast

Wait, no I didn't, the maids on holiday. I couldn't eat at home that's why I had to stop at the coffee shop. I ordered my cocoa-coffee (*which was cold...need to warm that up*). Got two cookies and...OMG, DID I LEAVE MY PHONE & CARD CASE ON THE COUNTER? It's times like these that I regret having glass walls in my office because I feel like falling on the floor and flailing around like a small child who was just denied an ice cream cone in the middle of the mall. Through sheer embarrassment I reach out to one of my most trusted employees *"Jasmine Green"*, she takes a second to pick up the phone and as soon as she hears the desperateness in my voice as I call out her name. "Erica, is that you...here I come girl". In a flash, maybe because the office isn't huge but instead an intimate boutique like setting where our clients feel more like family than clients...she enters (*without knocking*). "Erica Brown, you are looking too fly to be moping around here, did you break your heel or something, because I know your dog didn't eat your homework and I know damn good and well that it's not over a man" she stands there with her hands on her hips. Jasmine is a voluptuous woman with curves for days. I honestly couldn't even imagine her in a size six because her personality is too big for all of that and the delivery and execution of her words just wouldn't hold as much merit. "My phone" I manage to push out in a small whimper. Jasmine walks around to my desk and lifts my head "Girl shit, speak the hell up, you know I can't hear without my glasses. What the hell did you say"? She still treats me like she did when we were teenagers. She has always used tough love when it's come to me. She always said that I can talk the talk...but when it comes to walking the walk...I tend to lose my sense of direction. But trust me, you would NEVER know, because homie don't play that! As I look up to her with sad eyes I say again, "I lost my phone". She steps back and looks at me like I called her from up the street and her hamburger and fries got cold *or* I interrupted her in the middle of a nut. "I know that you are not in here whining over a phone, woman you have insurance, just get another one". Although she was correct and frankly it was an easy fix that I could just have Ashlyn correct over the phone; something just didn't feel right. "I know; you're right. I don't even know why I'm tripping" I was about to continue when the intercom buzzed and I was interrupted in mid-sentence. "Yes Ashlyn, what is it"? She always sounds so perky and that truly doesn't help when I'm feeling like this. "WHAT it is; is a message...WHO it is, that's what I would like to know". I leap from my desk and dash out my office and over to the reception area. Jasmine is close on my heels in anticipation to see who or what all of the fuss is about. I pump my breaks quickly as I approach the desk and PRAY that Jasmine does the same because her big ass will knock us all over and although I have GREAT insurance I'm not trying to use it. I don't believe Aflac will believe me if I told them that I got ran over by a dear friend...but there wasn't a car involved. As I approach the desk I see a single long stemmed pink rose with a small note card in a white envelope. "Where is the person that brought this" I asked Ashlyn as she sat grinning like the damn Cheshire cat? ". "Child that wasn't just a person...that was a GOD that dropped this off. I asked him to wait while I buzzed you but when I looked up...he was gone". Ashlyn looked guilty like she had just broken her mother's favorite vase. I did my best to hide my emotions and took the single rose and headed back to my office. I guess they both knew not to follow me, especially since I was going to end up telling them anyway. I walked over to the couch and sat down. I had no secret admirers so I honestly didn't know what to expect when I opened the card. I was shocked and this time I couldn't help but let my expression reveal what was happening inside my heart and head. Where in the hell did these butterflies come from? The card was well written short and to the point.

It read:

Dear Erica,

I guess I was right when I said that our paths would cross again. In your haste you apparently left your phone, business cards and lip gloss on the counter at the coffee shop. I would love to get these items back to you...and you personally. Please give me a call and let's pick a time and place to meet. Call me anytime 555-452-832

Edward Sparks

It's him, Mr. Always Free. I guess I know how he got my name and where to find me...my business card. I respect the pink rose, because red is way too personal when you don't KNOW me KNOW me! Although the

school girl in me wants to leave work NOW and run

home to start this little product recovery mission, I'm

a business woman first and I get back to doing what I

do best...fixing people and their broken relationships. I

have one more appointment today and then I can go

home and soak in my beautiful garden tub. I just

remembered again that my chef won't be there...I

wonder if I should cook tonight. You know what, I just

might do that.

Just as I was placing the card back in its envelope the

telephone number catches my attention. He forgot to

put the last digit; how in the hell am I supposed to get

in touch with him now? I remember as a young video

vixen I would give guys my number leaving off the last

number just to weed out those who weren't really

serious about getting in touch with me. I figured if you took the time to go through each number starting with zero then you were at least entitled to ONE date. As you see, I've always thought highly of myself, the way that I feel everyone should. Why do we leave the confidence trait to those who were born privileged and/or eye twitchingly unattractive? I'm sure you'll agree with me when I say, the world's most beastly looking people have THEE most confidence in the world. You have to darn near send a carrier pigeon over to an attractive guy to get his attention, but let an ugly... (*for lack of a better word...I'm sure there's a nicer word I could use, but as the legendary Bernie Mack said "Fuck em"*), back to what I was saying about those who are "attractively challenged" (*see I told you there was a nicer way to put it*). Get caught in the eye scope of an ugly man; that sucka will climb mountains, swim through alligator infested swamps

and fight his way through a plain of armed savages

just to walk ALL the way over to you JUST to get shot

down. Not to sound conceited BUT what in THEE hell

possessed you to take that trek from way over THERE

to way over HERE to approach someone that YOU

KNOW wouldn't give you the time of day even if she

had a watch on each wrist. I mean her FATHER could

be FATHER TIME and she still wouldn't find any time

for you! However, you have to love their endurance

and steadfast way of looking at life. But honestly

speaking, they may want to adjust the shade of those

rose colored lenses that they are looking through

because *"bay bay"* not on any given Sunday will you

get a chance to lay with me...sorry.

The more I look at this note and the more time I take to think about it I wonder…is this man playing a game with me now? I wonder if he thinks he's going to get a reward. I wonder if I should even offer a reward. Because honestly, I didn't leave it with him, so how did he get it? I will be speaking with management in the morning about their policy on their staff giving their customers other people's belongings. Oh yes, someone will be getting a strongly worded letter this week…strongly worded!

As I wrap up my last client for the day I grab my things and head for the elevator. When I exit the elevator I see that Ashlyn has already called ahead and my driver is waiting in front. God bless her, she probably feels that I'm so scatter brain today that I would get lost walking the seven blocks to my condo; and where my mind has been lately, she's probably right. I check to be sure that I grabbed all of my things...or at least what I currently have in my possession before I head home. Crazy "me" is still looking for my cell phone when my driver opens the car door and utters the words "Pink Rose ma'am". That quickly, I had totally forgotten that I didn't have my phone. "Thank you" *(embarrassingly I forgot his name...if I ever knew it to begin with).* "Justin ma'am" he said in a calm and respectful voice. "Thank you Justin. I need to stop at the CVS before I go in for the evening if you don't mind" I smiled and got into the car as I innocently ignore his hand to help me in *(that was a sheer mistake).* He closed the door and walked around to the driver side. Dressed in a black suit, white dress shirt and black tie; he removed his suit jacket and draped it on the passenger seat and sat down. He smelled refreshingly good to just be a driver. He either took great pride in the way he presented himself or he planned on using the company car to escort his lady out for the evening because there is just something very different about him today. Anyway, I thought him wanting to transport his lady in style was sweet and I had no problem with that; especially considering that it wasn't actually MY personal vehicle. I use an elite transportation service called "LUXE ELITE". They allow you to request the driver you want. When I started using the service I was only transported by the actual owner, a guy they call "Sunday **@luxeelite**; I'm still not sure that's what his mama named him, but oh well. Although he was an excellent transporter and bodyguard he was able to sit back and just chill once his business and clientele picked up. I continue to request Justin because he seems like such a sweet guy and since I have such a robotic schedule it allows him to work on any personal endeavors. See, even when it seems like I'm not paying attention or not in tune with things around me just know that my subconscious is working over-time. Hell, I look at it this way, I used to squeeze in special privileges and products from my former employers all of the time. I remember I used to work at the perfume counter in Hudson's at Northland Mall in Detroit, MI. while I was attending school. Needless to say that everyone received perfume that year for Christmas; and I smelled great EVERYDAY until my hot supply ran out. I'm sure you're looking at me like "oooh, she stole something". It was a HUGE corporation...*I don't give a shit*...they should have done a better background check. But hey, you never really know a person until it's too late; hell, I didn't know that I'd take it until the opportunity presented itself. Don't worry; I was the highest ranking sales person there; so technically I sold more than I stole, so bite me.

****

Inside the store I wander aimlessly around not remembering what I was supposed to be getting; which can be very dangerous if you're on a budget because you tend to just spend and spend…and most often, you're spending what you can't even afford to spend. I grabbed the normal medicine cabinet needs and my personal womanly products and head to the check out. The guy at the counter is an oddly handsome young man with horrid skin. I wish I would work IN a pharmacy type environment and NOT have flawless skin. He better tap into his *special privileges*, don't be crazy all your life! I wouldn't give two damns even if I had to open the LAST bottle in the back and put the shit on every morning. Because technically then it wouldn't be STEALING...I would just be SAMPLING their product. For whatever reason, I was feeling generous and asked for $100.00 cash back so that I could give my driver a surprise tip...for his date tonight. The young man politely explained to me that you couldn't get more than $50.00 back...so that's what I did. Oh well, I tried, sucks to be him. I exited the store and saw "Justin" (*see I remembered this time*) leaning against the car. Now that I looked again, he was a handsome guy...you know, for a driver I mean. I'm shocked that I never noticed that before. He opened the door like clockwork and closed it once I got back in.

As we pulled up to my condo, Justin opened the door, the night air hit me as did the smell of his sweet cologne. He reached for my hand and this time I allowed him to assist me. He asked sweetly if I'd like for him to walk me in. I simply said "No thank you, but thank you Justin", I handed him the $50.00 tip and told him to enjoy his date tonight. He uttered a most appreciative "Thank you" and you could tell that he wondered how I knew about tonight's big date. Let's just say that I'm great at reading people, as I said before, I'm good at what I do.

Once inside I kick off my shoes and although I know where they are supposed to go, I leave them right there; besides if they want to be in the closet so bad they can walk their little asses over there and jump on the shelf themselves...I'm tired. My mind is racing and the first thing I want to do is grab my cordless phone; yes, I am still one of the only people in the world who actually has a landline. Noticing how eager I am to hear this man's sultry voice again I halt my desires and decide to take a long hot bath. As I walk toward my bathroom I drop an article of clothing with each step. I always feel like I'm a Sharon Stone body double (*except with a better body*) when I do this. It feels as if cameras are rolling as my stride quickly turns into more of a stalking movement. My condo is adorned with floor to ceiling windows which remain uncovered by any type of curtains or shades. Don't worry, I'm not ground level, however, all above me truly get a hell of a show most nights. This is just another one of my contributions to modern society. I give the men something to dream about and the women something to strive for.

Once inside my bathroom I retrieve my bath oil from off of the vintage vanity tray located right next to my acrylic bathtub. The tub was designed by me after a dream. When I awoke from that dream I had a very good artist friend of mine named Andre **@artbyandre** recreate and produce this one of a kind four person bathtub. In the dream it didn't have a Jacuzzi feature, however, Andre was able to add it as a surprise feature; and I am so glad that he did. There is nothing like being able to soak in a bubble bath after a long day. He named the piece *(since it was a masterpiece)* "Calgon" which actually prompted him to develop an entire bathroom line. Needless to say he is making a killing off of the new line and my quarterly kickback sits nicely in my account since I was actually the MUSE or creative influence behind this product line. I live to be other people's inspiration; sometimes people just need a push...while others need a shove...and some just need to be knocked down a flight of stairs and out of the way of people who really want to succeed. "Move B#@%! get out the way"! Not being able to fight temptation anymore I reach for my cordless phone and the small piece of paper with Mr. Sparks'

number on it...and dial!

555-452-8320 (*Dialing*)

"Hello, my name is Erica Brown and I am trying to

reach Mr. Edward Sparks" I say in a very hesitant but

seductive voice. "Who is this" the unidentified woman

on the other end said in an almost irritated tone.

"Erica Brown, I'm not sure if I have the correct

number". "Naw, you ain't got the right number, how

you get my number anyway" she said but before she

could continue I abruptly cut her off and pressed the

end button on the phone. Some people are just so

ignorant.

555-452-8321 (*Dialing*)

"Joe's pool hall...eight ball speaking" he said in a

country voice. I didn't even converse with this "Duck

Dynasty" cast member. I simply said "wrong number" and kept it damn moving.

555-452-8322 (*Dialing*)

This time an older lady answered the phone. It took a minute for her to disconnect the external answering machine on her end and a few more seconds to actually release her first word. It appeared to be a scuffle on the other end and if you ask me I think the "phone" won. "Hello" she finally said in the sweetest voice you ever wanted to hear. It almost sound like she was on one of those old time machines that you used to stand on and place the belt around your waist. I think they were supposed to be for weight loss. Once you flipped the switch the motor roared and shook you so hard that you looked like you were having a damn seizure. I want to say that's where "twerking" actually started. "Um, yes, my name is Erica Brown and I was looking for Edward Sparks" I projected more loudly than before. I mean let's face it, she sounds like she's 122 years old. She probably has a hearing aid in her ear with a dead battery. She sounds so old that I'm sure she either knew Jesus personally or they dated on and off for three years. She begins to speak again "Edward you said, oh hold on baby". I can hear her put the phone down and begin to call out his name. I knew it...I damn knew it; this man lives with his grandmother! Not only do you NOT have a job, you are writing your name on the orange juice and living in your granny's basement. It takes her about four minutes to come back to the phone and I feel so sorry for her because she sounds winded and exasperated from going to tell him that the phone was for him. She says, "I'm sorry baby, I don't know what I was thinking...there's no Edward that lives here. I stay by myself". YOU OLD BAG OF BONES...NO YOU DIDN'T just have me hold for NO DAMN REASON while you go look for someone who never actually existed? I should find out where you live and come grease your floors you crazy old fool! Instead I said' Oh, that's no problem, sorry to bother you, you have a wonderful night ma'am". I hang up without even waiting for a response. I refuse to dial another wrong number without at least a drink in my hand. A cocktail will help me simmer down some because these people are working my last nerve and I don't even damn drink! I climb out of the tub and because I always add my "Pussy Bath Oil" to my bath water I don't have to worry about applying lotions because I'm already shinning from my soak. This "Pussy" smells so good. Oh, the bath oil, not mine. Well wait, let me rephrase that, I don't want you thinking that mine stinks or something…I just wasn't talking about it at this moment. I hope I cleared that up. Anyway, I have a monthly supply of bath and lotion products shipped to me from a company called "Heavenly Body" **@heavenlybodyproducts** located in Decatur, GA. I have my favorite scent infused into the oils, lotions, spray and candles. I'm normally stuck on "Pussy" but every now and then I may switch it up. Often times I will have them create a signature gift set when I meet a new man or if I have males that I need to give gifts to. I just love a good smelling man!

As I dry off I can't help but admire myself in my custom Swarovski Crystals encrusted floor length mirror. I had it imported from France after seeing it in a small boutique while vacationing there a couple of years back. The huge body towel engulfs my curvaceous figure as I slowly blot myself dry. You should avoid rubbing your skin dry because it removes most of the moisture that was intended to be left there after applying your particular body oil. You should always compare yourself to the finest things in life…because that is indeed what you are. While I continue to dry off I always refer back to the scene in "American Gangster" when the honorable Denzel Washington delivers his famous line "That's twenty-five thousand dollar Alpaca, you blot that shit, you don't rub it". Not to compare myself to an animal…but baby when it comes to drying off, I'm an Alpaca…you blot this shit! Getting dressed for bed is probably one of the easiest things in the world. I walk over to my vanity area and sit down in front of my mirror. This has to be one of my favorite pieces in my entire home. I don't want you to think that I am a label whore and completely materialistic, because I'm not. I would much rather give a starving artist my hard earned

money before I continue to support a famous

designers' lifestyle who has already made it. This

vanity was actually designed by a girl that I went to

high school with by the name of Sonya

@twisted_vixen. She is an avid thrifter and dumpster

diver. After she finds something, which could possibly

be sitting on the street; she takes it home, cleans it

up, changes the fabric, and adds her pizazz then

viola...a brand new OOAK (*one of a kind*) piece you

have. She is phenomenal at what she does. As often

as my schedule allows I join her on her *"Junk in the*

Trunk" thrifting excursions. It's a humbling and

creative experience. The vanity was in shambles and

barely standing *(mainly because it only had three*

legs); but there was something about it that caught

my eye and called out to me. The details adorned on it

were so elegant and elegantly crafted as it leaned in a dusty corner at the Goodwill Center over off Ponce De Leon. At that time I wasn't completely the risk taker that you see before you now. I had not yet opened my third eye to see beyond the surface of people, places and things. It took Sonya to bring it out of me. Through her eyes and explorations I learned to look at the beauty of things even when the surface was less than appetizing. It's crazy the lessons that life teaches us. Who would have guessed that you could learn a major life lesson by thrifting? Once you open your third eye you'll be amazed at just how much you can learn...but enough on that right now. I rise from my vanity and pass my closet because as I said, getting ready for bed is the easiest part of my day, because I sleep in the nude. Us Aquarians need to feel free at all times. So, naked, at least one foot from under the cover and single is the life we lead. That's at least until we drop our guard and learn to let someone in.

I walk to my gourmet open concept kitchen with hidden appliances to grab a bottle of "Pink Chardonnay" and a wine glass. Finding the glasses is easy due to the open shelving system that fits perfectly in the space. What is not so easy is locating the corkscrew. I rummage through three drawers before I finally find the darn thing that is actually sitting within arm's reach of the wine cellar, go figure. If it had been a snake...well, you know the rest. Luckily it's one of those motorized corkscrew that I actually found in the SKY MALL magazine on one of my many business trips. All you do is place it securely over the bottle top and it does the rest, leaving behind not even a trace of cork residue. Sutter House really hit a homerun when they came up with this one. It's not one of those *"it's a good year"* bottles of wine, it simply tastes sweet and not dry...and for that, I thank them. I'm not a heavy drinker unless you want to see a heavy sleeper a few minutes later. I simply like girly, soft and weak tasting things. I was a "Hunch Punch" kind of girl back in high school because it masked the taste of the liquor...which in all honesty is actually not good at all. Behind a faux cabinet door sits a massive and stocked to the max Thermador refrigerator. My housekeeper knows that I have a junk food worm in me that surfaces after eight o'clock every night. When it comes to snacks I swear I'm like a kid. Growing up we didn't have two nickels (*although we did have food stamps*) to rub together, so snacks, extra-curricular activities and all of the things that we actually WANTED were null and void. I take that back, every blue moon our mom would splurge on an array of box candy. Back in the day, when penny candy was exactly

that, we would all walk to the corner store,

"Fletcher's", where our mom would let us go HAM!

We would spend almost $20.00 in food stamps on box

candies and other goodies. When we got home she

would grab a big plastic mixing bowl from the kitchen

and we would spend the next several minutes

emptying each individual box of Cherry Clan's,

Alexander the Grape, Johnny Appleseed's, Boston

Baked Beans, Lemon Heads, Fruit Cocktails (*my*

freaking favorite) and Jaw Breakers into this bowl.

However, that was probably one of the only moments

in my dining memory that I care to remember.

Outside of that walking into our kitchen you would

have thought that you had traveled back in time (*in TV*

land) when all things were black and white. We used

to go to this place in Detroit called "Focus Hope" to

get our monthly source of food. However, the choices there were all packaged in plain and generic boxes and bags. Picture this, a dull white main layer with two bold black stripes going across it. If it was cereal you knew it by the word CEREAL on the front on the package, or MEAT or BEANS. The surprise was what kind once you actually opened it up. Our mother was a master at turning mush into a meal. When we ran out of the Focus Hope food we would have her infamous "Boiled Chicken and Rice". I vowed that if I ever grew up and was able to decide what I ate…a boiled chicken would NEVER cross my road! I grabbed the gallon version of "Strawberry Shortcake" from the freezer and found my favorite cup/bowl that was given to me by one of my favorite aunts. At the time that I got this cup/bowl I was infatuated with cats, so of course the ideal gifts were always adorned with cute little kitties all over everything. I fill my cup up with the delicious strawberry ice cream...probably more than what I need, but then again I'm unsupervised right now, almost anything is possible. I walk over to my oversized couch in the living room and place my glass, the bottle of wine, my cordless phone and bowl of ice cream down on the matching ottoman.

I took the faux fur throw from off the ottoman and placed it over my naked body as I sipped from my glass. I had already started writing my next relationship book *"You Got em', Now what are you Gonna do with em'"*, but then I remembered that I was on a mission to get back what was taken from me. Well, what I left on the counter at the coffee shop, but that's neither here nor there. I ignored the "You've Got Mail" notification from my laptop and picked back up my cordless phone. "Where was I", the words escaped my lips as I reconvened.

555-452-8323 (*Dialing*)

Before I could utter a single word that voice that has probably been heard by every single person in the world came in and said (*in her most pleasant tone*)…"The number you have reached 555-452-8323 has been disconnected. No further information will be given about 555-452-8323. Her voice is so soothing and calming that it should be used for several different things. Her tone could change a dark situation into a day of rainbows. I would have her call in for me to quit a job if I could. Her voice alone would probably have them put a bonus on my last check. Her voice should be on the recording if you could call in and get your test results from the doctor. You'd almost be able to accept it if she told you that you had herpes and the gout. I have never really understood the reason for her saying "No further information will be given", like really, what else can be said? Is she going to tell us WHY their phone was cut off or maybe give us an alternate number for them?

555-452-8324 (*Dialing*)

I top my glass of wine off again (*for the third time*) and get back to the nature at hand. The voice that picked up was very sultry and sexy and for a quick second my heart began to race. I think I found him and it feels like someone just "Control-ALT-Deleted my entire vocabulary. The words are swirling around in my mind when all of a sudden it's interrupted by "Sike, I got you, we're not home right now, but if you want to reach Jason, J'me or James" leave a message and someone will return your call...or nah". It was followed by laughter and barking. Friggin Q-dogs irritate the inside of my asshole! But I smile

anyway...they got me.

555-452-8325 (*Dialing*)

"Hello" the voice was deep and erotic. Again, it

sounded like it could be him, but I damn sure wasn't

going to fall for the banana in the tailpipe. I waited for

another "Hello" but was still skeptical because I knew

how immature and stupid people could be. Just as I

got the confidence to say something the line went

dead. I guess it was the real deal Holyfield and not an

answering machine as I suspected. Just as I was about

to dial the number back my phone rang in my hand

almost giving me a small heart attack. I didn't have to

guess who it was because the name was digitalized

across the screen of the cordless phone. So, the magic

number FIVE it is!

ADVICE #122

Ladies and Gents, let me help you save some time

when finding a new mate. The next time you meet

someone try this...**DO NOT** look for the things that you

LIKE; instead seek out the things that you simply will

NOT ACCEPT! This should help you weed out those

who will do nothing but waste your time. Remember,

you can get just about ANYTHING back...however,

once TIME is gone...TIME is gone! Unless of course

your name is Marty and you were in *"Back to the*

Future". Then by all means, jump in your 81' DeLorean

and try it again. But in the real world we know that's

simply NOT possible. So, set your watches accordingly

because..."*Ain't nobody got time for that*"!

Chapter Three

The Best of the Worst

I decided to meet him at the coffee shop where the theft took place, that way I can speak to the manager about their policy on other people's personal belongings. I get there about fifteen minutes early so that I can see him walk; that's one thing that I don't recall catching the other day. The way a man walks says a lot about him. If he walks with his shoulders slumped over like he's almost trying to disappear then be careful, more than likely, he is. However, a man walking upright and confident can be a very good look. A straight back and chin up means confidence and that he commands respect when he enters a room. Please keep in mind that there is an extreme difference between a person with their chin up and a person with their nose in the air; this goes for men and women. More than likely that person believes that their worth is higher than yours and if that is the case let that fool walk on by. You don't need anyone who will make you feel inferior or the feeling that you are in constant competition with each other. Now, a fun and innocent competition is just fine, especially if it pushes YOU to be a better YOU!

I don't order my usual today, instead I grab a ham and cheese croissant and a lemon and orange infused spring water. I don't need brown teeth when I meet

"Mr. Return to Sender".

It feels like I've been waiting forever but when I look down at my watch (*since I don't have my phone*) I see that in all actuality only five minutes have passed.

When I look back up standing in front of me is what appears to be a male runway model in subtle charcoal gray dress pants and black cashmere V-neck sweater. I see a white t-shirt peeking out from beneath his sweater which only tells me that his mama raised him right. Today he is wearing black leather Louis Vuitton loafers (*no penny*) that almost appear to be new. He is hovering over me smiling with that same Colgate smile. Although fully clothed you can see the outline of his muscles and that is currently doing something to me. I know that it really doesn't matter, but for all of those who are interested I see NO RING and NO RING TAN LINE! But then again, who is rushing to marry someone who can't bring home the bacon. Hell, if I have to bring home the bacon AND cook it, then damn it, I'm eating it by my damn self...

ALL OF IT!

"Good morning Ms. Brown, thank you so much for accepting my offer for breakfast this morning. You are looking spectacular as usual" he says with a grin that can melt butter. I am not falling for these high school games so he can save his breath and that smile. I am glad that I chose to wear my new low cut pencil dress which made his view from up there pleasurable. The little old lady that brings to life the fashion visions in my mind must have hit the bottle early on the day that she designed this dress because somehow she misread the instructions and made the split too high and the "V" too low...but today I internally smile when I see now that it turned out to be the perfect mishap. Ms. Mary always said that "there is a method to my madness". I found this beautiful fabric on Ebay that had sexy pin-up girls all over it, just like in the magazines back in the day. I complimented the busy pattern of the dress with a basic (*but stylish*) shoe and clutch. A vibrant yellow peep toe shoe with a five inch heel; the clutch looked retro with it's over sized button on the closing clasp.

I stare for a minute before my brain tells my vocal cords to release my captive words. "Good morning Mr. Sparks, the pleasure is all mine. Would you like to sit down and discuss more of this delusion that you have about us going to breakfast...because for some reason I didn't get the memo"? My smirk was playful and with that being said...he continued to play along. "Oh well maybe that was just me and my wishful thinking" he said as he took a seat. His long limbs found mine underneath the table as they brushed past my soft legs that I had crossed at the ankle. Before I could ask he placed my phone, card case and Mac lip gloss on the table. I smirked and said "thank you" as I placed them into my sunny clutch. He began speaking "So, I guess I will ask you this time. Would you make my day and accompany me for breakfast this morning"? I didn't see the harm in it except for the fact that I had already ordered my ham and cheese croissant. After I told him that I had already ordered he quickly got up from the table and walked over to the counter to speak to the young male cashier. I don't know what was said, all I knew was that he was back standing at the table with his hand extended and simply replied "You're all set, you have a credit now. Just order it when you come in next time. Now, may we go?" I softly took hold of his powerful hand as he easily lifted me to my feet. There was no reason for us to be standing as closely as we were, but if he wasn't complaining...neither was I. Our body heat and chemistry could be seen a mile away.

Seriously, the distance that we shared was of two people standing in a crowded elevator with no room to even turn around. When he released my hand I took two steps back so that my blood could begin to flow correctly. Because you know that in order for your blood to flow your heart has to be beating. For some reason this man causes me to hold my breath which in turn stops my heart and leaves me mentally, physically and emotionally vulnerable and for the TAKING! There, that's my excuse, the fine print, my final answer, my disclosure or whatever else you want to call it when I find myself sleeping with this man before noon today. I scientifically was not ABLE to WITHSTAND the pressure due to heart failure. Now, where was I? I don't even know where we are going as he leads me to and out the double glass doors. Before we exit he waves to a few of the employees. He must have been a regular here before he decided to start working there. This must be his "Cheers" just without the alcohol. Makes sense, what better place to work at than someplace where everybody knows your name.

"I know this really nice quaint spot just around the corner if you are up to a three block walk" he said as he pointed in the direction going deeper into the Atlanta downtown area. Although the shoes that I had on were not exactly "walking shoes" they were quite comfortable and the weather was oddly beautiful for an early April day". Georgia weather can be all over the place sometimes, you never know what you're in store for. Most of the times even the weather person looks shocked as they deliver the news.

"It's a little spot called "Jus Jazzy's" **@spazz_i_am** and the food is wonderful. Honestly it's my niece's spot and I'm always for supporting family whenever I can"

he concluded. I should have known that he'd find

someplace where he could get the hookup. We

walked silently and I pulled out my

phone...damn...dead! Common sense would have told

him to turn it off....common sense. He was probably

up all night jacking off to my nude pictures. Silly me,

refuses to put a code on my cell phone; for one,

because I have nothing to hide from anyone, and for

two...I'd probably have to reset it every day because

I'd more than likely forget the password. I slipped my

phone back into my purse as we walked in silence

taking in the sights. There are so many colorful

characters in downtown Atlanta. I'm sure that every

city has its fair share of unique "rent-free" individuals

BUT Atlanta takes the cake. When I used to work for a

company centralized in downtown Atlanta, I would

often come outside and eat my lunch in the park and

"People watch" (*one of the BEST past times in the*

world). I would sit for hours (*often pass my scheduled*

lunch hours and just let my mind wander). Many times

I would imagine where people were going, what

secret rendezvous they were coming from or heading

to and more than anything I would look at the

homeless men and women and wonder who they

once were and what catastrophic event caused them

to end up where they are now. Sometimes I believe

that where I am right now (*and please keep in mind*

that it is a VERY comfortable place) is not actually

where God intends for me to ultimately end up...more

on that later.

We turn onto Peachtree St. and run smack dab into a

line of food trucks and there in the mix of the fray sits

a huge truck with zebra stripes on it but the stripes

are actually words; it's pretty neat. Edward reaches over the crowd standing in front of the truck and grabs a menu and hands it to me. "What do you suggest because I could eat just about anything right now" I say. Instead of giving me his suggestion he actually says "You know what, let's ask the chef what she suggests". We avoid fighting the line at the window (*like she's selling the new "Jordan's" or something in there)* but instead we walk to the door and he knocks; what I assume to be a signature knock. When the door opens I see a very pretty little girl who is probably no more than fourteen years old. I love to see kids working early because it teaches them values and the importance of creating a solid working foundation and understanding finance.

She smiles as she says "What up doe' cuz, you want the usual"? Maybe this is his cousin's daughter...family helping family...B-E-A utiful! He smiles and quickly I notice the resemblance. "Actually, I want you to meet someone and you tell us what is the best thing on the menu today; Erica this is my cousin Ny'Chole and this is her food truck *"Jus Jazzy Cafe"*. This man has me confused for the day. This is a child that I'm meeting right now...right? I'm guessing she saw the bewilderment on my face because she smiled what has to be a family trait (*a great smile*) and says "I'm twenty one...I just look twelve. Although my cousin is trying me this morning like there's actually something on my menu that is NOT good, today's special is a "Cajun Shrimp and Chicken Pasta inside of a bread bowl"; it's actually one of my best sellers and Edward's favorite". I smile because it sounds and smells wonderful. I do have to warn her though..."I am allergic to shellfish so if I can get it without the shrimp that would be great". She winks at Edward as she smiles and says "Oh, lookie here, we have another shellfish allergy". She yells over her shoulder to one of the prep cooks. "Two Cajun Chicken and Pasta bowls" before she looks back at us. "Your food will be coming right up. You guys can sit over there and someone will bring it out to you. Give me about fifteen minutes". She closes the door and I follow *"Mr. I Got the Hook-up"* over to a small two-seater table under a tree. I would be lying if I said that I wasn't intrigued by this man. I'm not sure what it is but I think that there is more than meets the eye with him. He brushes my seat off and places one on the linen napkins on the seat chair that I assume he picked up when he grabbed the menus. "I hope this is to your liking my lady" he smirks as he pulls my chair out. "It's just fine, thank you very much. I hope you have good taste when it comes to food" I teased. "My taste in food and clothes is nothing compared to my taste in women" he proclaimed with a sinister grin. I don't know who this boy thinks HE is playing with but I will put a hurting on him something awful, he better play with someone on his own damn level. "I've been going to that coffee shop for years now, it's funny that I've never seen you, I think I would have remembered that" I said and before he could chime in I cut him off. "I'm not trying to blow your head up or anything but you are very easy on the eyes if I say so myself".

"What's wrong with blowing someone's head"...I don't even hear the word up because my mind has went totally in the gutter and I visualize me kneeling in front of him as I devour his manhood right here in the middle of this park as a shocked and intrigued audience looks on. Not to toot my own horn but I could teach the birds and bees a few things my damn self! I come to, as I catch the tail end of the conversation, fuck it, I'll make the rest up that I missed later on. "I'm a firm believer in giving people their roses while they are still alive. What good is a compliment once they're gone" he said in the most serious tone to date. "I couldn't agree with you more Mr. Sparks" I announced just before our food came to the table. Ny'Chole approached the table in her black and white checked pants, black tank top and white apron. "Here you go, I hope you both enjoy it and since you didn't say what you wanted to drink I took it upon myself to add two large sweet teas...the Jazzy way that is" she said as she placed everything on the table and began to walk away. "Oh, once you're done I will send out dessert...trust me, you'll love it as well" she added before she disappeared inside the zebra food truck. She is cute as a button. Their family has great genes...maybe we'll swap DNA later...maybe.

The wind blows and in the air there is a mixture of all of the different aromas from the dozen or so food trucks. I know that I should be overwhelmed by the numerous smells but honestly the only thing that I can smell is the pasta bowl in front of me and whatever this man is wearing today. "Mr. Sparks" I sang before I was quickly cut off. "Please call me Edward, Erica" he requested. "My apologies, Edward, your taste in food is phenomenal and if I didn't think she'd slap me across my face I'd march right up there and kiss your cousin square in her mouth. I mean this is delicious! I think I will use her for my next event because I am completely sold" I said. I normally don't mind people staring at me...hell I've been starred at all of my life. But when I look up and see Edward glaring at me there is something more behind his eyes. "Can I help you with something Edward" I said, not really sure if I was ready for his response. "It all depends; how far can my request stretch" he replied with a sexy grin as he bit his lip. In my mind I believe what he is really trying to say is "How far can my legs stretch" and if that's the case, then the answer is, behind my head and into a full split...both ways...regular and Chinese. Now, who's your daddy? But instead of falling into his little web I keep it on track and in a controlled atmosphere as I simply reply with "You'll never know until you ask". He shy's away turning that handsome face away from me. When he turns back around he blurts out feverishly in a "now or never" manner "Well, let's see how well my luck continues today. Can I see you again (*wait for it*) tonight? I know it's last minute and I'm probably pushing my luck...but, like you said, I'll never know if I don't ask". I am sitting

here acting like someone not use to being pursued. I

can't believe that I'm smitten by this man and I don't

know anything about him except for the fact that I'll

probably be footing the bill or we'll pull the old "Dine

and Ditch". When I hear me utter the words "I'd be

delighted" I almost choke on them. I haven't even

checked my calendar to make sure that I'm even free.

His smile melts my soul as it flows downwardly

towards my mid-section. The liquid which was once

my soul and the buildup of my creamy sexual desire

would now be saturating my panties...if I was wearing

some. I swear it never fails, it is virtually impossible to

hold a conversation without my signature sarcasm

showing up and stealing the show. "So, does Ny'Chole

have a dinner menu or does your uncle own a hot dog

stand nearby"? As quickly as I say it, I just as quickly

wish I could have caught it before I let it escape. To my surprise he begins to laugh until tears come into his eyes. "You are quick with that little tongue of yours Ms. Brown. For your information YES she does have an outstanding dinner menu and while you got jokes, I actually do have an uncle that owns a hotdog cart called "That's My Dog"; but he's on the west coast. I'm not sure how long your lunch break is". Need I remind this man that it is MY signature at the bottom of the checks that "I" send out bi-weekly to over 23 employee's #ithankyou. If I had been ten years younger I would have called his damn bluff and went to go get that hot dog off the West Coast...smart ass! "Well actually that hot dog sounds good. Where did you park your private jet again" I say? He smiles and replies as he moves in closer and all I can think is, boy I'm BLIND not DEAF...but proceed because he smells almost good enough to eat...or at least lick on

for a few hours. When he speaks I get the hint of

cinnamon; someone uses "Close Up". "I'll assume

you're just joking, but I'll keep that in mind for maybe

our second date". He looks deep into my eyes and

he's so friggin close that our noses almost brush. "I

was thinking that maybe I can cook for you this

evening...if that works for you". I catch my breath

AND his too since he's just about down my throat

right now *(NOT complaining)*. I decide to just jump

right in and volunteer my gourmet kitchen because at

this point in this social venture I want to continue this

little game we're playing; even if it is just my

imagination that is creating this man to be some kind

of God. He probably doesn't have a pot to piss in or a

window to throw it out. It's my fantasy and as long as I

can it will be played out by my rules. I'm not ready to

see his one bedroom apartment with bargain basement furniture. Before you get your panties in a knot or boxers in a bunch, I'm not judging, we all have dreams and desires and I have fought my way up out the swallows of this world and right now I'd prefer my man already perfectly seasoned. I don't have time for another project...hell; I'm a work in progress myself.

I'll be working on me for the rest of my life!

****

I don't know what I was expecting as the sun set and the moon danced across the downtown Atlanta sky. He called a couple of hours ago and asked me if I had any allergies or specific food dislikes...that was thoughtful. Growing up we didn't have the luxury of being able to have a favorite food. You ate what was in front of you for dinner...or you ate it for breakfast. A word of advice: If ever presented with this option "eat it for dinner...the first night". Our other option (*our mother always gave us an option*); "You can eat it or you can wear it". I never said they were the BEST choices in the world. I just said she never left us without options. We quickly learned the expression "The lesser of two evils". Edward told me to not do anything and that he will bring the groceries...cook the groceries and if need be feed the groceries to me! Well sweet baby Jesus, he must be trying to get him some tonight. No really, let me get myself together. I guess I'm supposed to be dressing down since this is a stay at home dinner. However, the closest thing I have to casual Friday's is my birthday suit and although I'm quite sure that he would be pleased with the details on that garment, I think I'll wait to pull out "this old thing" as my mother used to say whenever she walked into our old house with fancy new duds...LOL!

I keep candles burning in my place on a daily basis so today is no different. I just hope he likes the fragrance. I've already prepared myself for him to pull a real nigga move and bring take-out, already prepared by those who do it best...a chef. I give myself a once over to make sure that everything is as close to perfection as I can muster without my glam squad. I was going to swing by my girls spot to get my tresses done, but my master stylist Shanna Anise **@redmystiqueart** was on set of a reality show. Did this chick not understand that I was about to be making camera worthy moves tonight myself. That's the only downfall of having a celebrity stylist. She is a beast at what she does; so I'll give her a pass just this once. Sitting in the park left my hair smelling like outdoors and the farmers market with all of those different smells. I just decided to wash it and let the curls fall where they may. I'd like to thank my mom

and dad for the decent strands of hair coming out of

my head. Some days I don't know what I would have

done without you. I decided to go with a pair of silk

joggers and a cut off top that showed off my tummy.

The shirt read "You'll NEVER be able to afford me...but

we can discuss a PAYMENT PLAN". This shirt is actually

from a line of shirts that I created called "Dis-Fuk-U-

nah" (*dysfunctional*) Tees. I designed shirts that

hopefully answered people's questions before they

even made the mistake of approaching me. I "used" to

be a bitch! I mean, I still am, but it's more watered

down. What best describes that is one of my other

shirts that read: 333 I'm Only Half Evil"...LMAO! I

don't care if I'm going to the Mayors Ball or the

mailbox my undies will ALWAYS match. What if I get

hit by a car and have to be taken to the hospital

unconscious? What if by some crazy twist of fate I walk over one of those manholes and my dress takes flight? You gotta be ready for anything my dears.

I was so caught up admiring myself in the mirror that I don't know how many times the doorbell rang. It seemed to mix perfectly well with "Beyoncé's" "Drunk in Love" that was blaring from the surround sound speakers. I almost break my neck running to the door; tripping over the huge area rug that I have covering the floor. I catch my composure right before I press the button for the intercom. "Hello" I say as I try to mask the rapid sound of my breathing. I swear when he finally speaks it feels like I've tuned into one of those late night R&B stations where the DJ sounds like his voice was crafted and tuned by God himself. The good thing about this "hey Mr. DJ" is that I know that the looks fall right in line with the voice. Most radio

DJ's are behind the speaker for a reason and that is because the majority of them look like the fifth "Teenage Mutant Ninja Turtle". So ugly that they need to go back in their shell and seal it shut, indefinitely. That's mean...I know, but isn't it mean that you would present that face to the rest of humanity? I mean so ugly that it looks like they were born on Halloween.

Okay, that's enough of that. "If it wasn't such a beautiful night I'd be in my feelings for you keeping me waiting for so long" he said. His chastising voice was even sexy...DAMN! "Please forgive me Edward, I promise I will make it up to you" I say before I push the button to unlock the gate. Since I own the entire building I don't have to worry about nosey neighbors all up in my business of who I'm "courting".

When the elevator arrives at the loft floor and the gates part he walks out looking like an Armani model.

He is wearing some distressed jeans (*not tight like the rest of these "so-called-men"*); baggy enough to offer comfort (*but not hanging around his knees like he's advertising anal sex*). He has on a plain white t-shirt with some white shell-toe Adidas. Not everyone can dress down and still look like a million bucks. I remove the two brown paper grocery bags from his arms and attempt to head to the kitchen; but not before he stops me. He steals a hug and kisses me on the forehead and politely takes the bags back from me. "Little lady I thought that I told you that tonight is all about you. Allow me to be a complete gentleman tonight. Now if you can guide me to the kitchen I can get this thing started". I take the hint as I sashay over to the kitchen. "What do you need...pot and pans wise" I say before he just runs through that open door. "I need for you to come and sit your sexy little self, right here" as he leads me to the high back stool seated in the center of the circular custom island. I have no problem being an audience member for this self-proclaimed Next Top Chef. Hell, let's just go full force with this thing. I can act like I don't have any arms and you can just feed my ass. Chew the shit up and put it in my mouth why don't you. No, let me stop before I throw up even thinking about it. I don't too much even like swapping spit these days...my foreplay days are over. I have become hardened in my old age.

"So, what's on the menu for tonight Edward" I ask as I run my finger around the gold plated rim of my Waterford China glass. "You'll just have to wait and see pretty lady. You have a beautiful home Erica. Did you decorate it yourself" he asked. "I will answer every question you have, but only if you allow me to help you" I said as I rose off the stool and walked over to the kitchen sink where I had the new hands-free Kohler faucet put in. I love it and with the new smart home technology it knows what you need almost before you do. As I approach the sink the water automatically turn on the correct temperature so that I can wash my hands. "Now that's something I've never seen before and I thought I saw it all" Edward stated as he walked up behind me to get a better look. I could feel his body heat and it was intoxicating. If I don't get this man off my back and fast, I'll need to rewet my hair, because it is about to straight frizz up. I squirmed out of the way and walked over to the counter to start removing the items from the bag. With each item removed it's starting to look like it's going to be an AWESOME night! He went to "Whole Foods" (*more than likely a hook-up*) and went ham! He had two porter house boneless steaks, large organic sweet potatoes, fresh spinach and plenty of different veggies and seasonings. "So, what can I do first my good man, I am completely at your disposal" I said as I moved to the cabinet to remove my strainer. "If you don't mind washing off the spinach and cutting up the vegetables...you could do that" he reached over my head to reach for the skillet that was hanging from the wrought iron pan rack suspended over the counter. I began to rinse off the things in my area when he hit me with the Q&A. "So, why is such a beautiful woman NOT taken? I would think you would have a line of suitors standing outside your door. I won't front, when I first saw you, I couldn't help but think of you in inappropriate ways. I mean, if we're going to start this friendship off honestly. Within the first few seconds I pictured you in a bikini and a wedding dress". He leaned over to me and in almost a whisper said "I'm not trying to scare you...just stating the facts ma'am". I'm not a pervert or anything, just a man with an active and stimulating mental pallet. I just don't want you to look at me in the wrong light". I believe that I have heard it all so nothing actually has "Shock Value" anymore to me. I told you, I have become unbothered and desensitized. "Don't worry, you're fine. I'd be lying if I didn't say that I didn't picture you lying across my bed when I first saw you".

He nearly cut his finger off after I said it, but recovered quickly, "its human nature and most of the time I am human" I said with a seductive giggle. He laughed and repeated my question back to me "Most of the time you're human, what are you the other half of the time"? "Depending on who I'm with...I could be damn near an animal" I said. That last statement must have did it, because the nick that he had started on

his finger a few minutes ago had turned into a cut. I
rushed to him to assist but he moved even quicker
than me. He rushed over to the sink and ran his
fingers under the streaming water. I walked up behind
him and placed his massive hands into mine as I
doctored on him and placed a Band-Aid on his finger
that I retrieved from the drawer behind him. "It's not
even that bad, I better not see a tear" I joked. He
laughed and pulled me into him as he gazed into my
eyes "How do you know that I didn't do it on purpose
just for this very moment"? "Because if you don't
know by now that I already had the entertainment for
this evening mapped out in my head...and actually had
already made the decision that you were a candidate
to get some, then you shouldn't even be here", I
turned his hand over and kissed the back of it and
walked away. I already knew that he was standing

there trying to come up with the most perfect response. However, instead of trying to match my gangsta he went in a completely different direction. "Erica, let's play a game" he casually said. "I love games, what did you have in mind" I responded as I started to walk over to my game cabinet. "No, not any board game that you have here...something I made up" he replied in a sneaky and sexy tone. I could already feel that this was something that could ultimately get me in trouble, but anyone who knows me knows that I can't turn down a challenge or dare. "It's something like truth or dare, but with a twist" he said. "I'm intrigued...continue" I stated. "Well it's an ice breaker game, all you have to do is answer the question honestly, and swiftly, the first thing that comes to mind, no cheating. However, if you don't answer you have to give the other person a KISS,

somewhere on their body, the location is completely
your choice OR remove an article of clothing" he
smirked and winked like he had just come up with the
game of the century. "Sounds like fun, I'm an open
book so don't be too surprised if you don't get any
action" I responded back with a wink.

The steaks were broiling while the spinach was
sautéing. I added the onions and mushrooms to the
spinach as he added some spices that I couldn't make
out because it didn't have a label on it. This damn man
could be a serial killer and I could be his next victim.
He might be trying to "Jeffery Dahmer" me or
something. That would be horrible. But I'm hungry,
for the steak AND the sausage so it is what it is...so be
it!

"First question, Erica, when was the last time you
were in love" he asked. "I'm in love now, as we

speak…with myself. I have yet to find anyone that can love me the way I do" I retorted. "Okay, that's a fair response, but you never know, you may have just met someone who can love you BETTER than you can. I think that would be the ultimate goal…wouldn't you say" he replied. He's a slick one and I must say I like that. I'd rather a man seduce my mind before anything else. "I guess it's my turn…Edward, did you think you were going to get lucky with me tonight" I said. "Honestly, yes, I did…and before you "Turn up on a Tuesday", it wasn't because I think you're easy. It's because the sexual tension between us was undeniable. I could also tell that you are a woman who doesn't play around or one who would let an opportunity pass her by. So basically, I knew that we both wanted each other" he explained. "Ms. Brown, why did you run away from me when we first met, what scared you off" he continued. I wasn't sure if this was a two part question and if this was even legal, however, you won't get anywhere arguing with the "maker" of the game. He could change the rules at any time and I would be none the wiser. I was debating if I would be completely honest or if I would remix the truth. I mean, it would still be the truth, just being delivered through rose colored lenses. But after three glasses of red wine, the truth slid its ass right on out. "Honestly Edward, I had already undressed you and had your baby within the first sixty seconds of seeing you" I take a deep breath "But when I saw you standing there with that application in your hand, it was just a turn off. I have dated too many frogs in my life and I believe that I have made enough major strides to where I no longer have to settle". I didn't even want to look at this face because I think I just hurt his feelings with the whole "Princess and the Frog" comparison. Luckily for me his back was turned to me because he was retrieving the steaks out of the oven. "We are talking about when you saw me in the coffee shop...right" was his only comeback. "Yes, and I apologize if I hurt your feelings, but it's your game and you asked for the truth" I said. When he turned to face me he just stood back and glared at me, crossing his arms over that broad chest of his. "So what made you change your mind and give little old me a chance" he said.

"There's just something about you that intrigues me. You have a mysterious air about yourself and I like mysteries" I replied. "So, you mean to tell me that you're okay if I'm just a blue collar guy trying to find his place in life" he questioned me like I was being interrogated. "I'm saying that I'd just like to see where this goes. I'm not a sugar momma or an enabler and I'm not looking for a pool boy...BUT...I can appreciate someone in their building stage. Would I prefer that you have at least as much as me, hell yeah? But it's not like we're about to get married or anything. We are just testing the waters, having fun".

"That's interesting" he said as I placed the plates on the counter next to his massive arms. "On a scale from one to ten, ten being the BEST, how would you rate your KISS...OVERALL BEDROOM SKILLS...and ORAL SKILLS"? A smile escaped as he asked the questions. I laughed because he thinks he's slick. "Bastard, how many turns do you think you're going to take" I said. "You're right, that was my bad, but since you JUST used your question on asking me that...it's my turn again. We both laughed because regardless of how unfair that was...it was the truth. I see now that he can't be trusted, so I have to watch him. He grabs both plates as we walk over to the dining area. "We can actually sit out on the balcony since it's such a nice night" I suggested. "I'll follow you wherever you want me to go" he said. Well homie if it's like that we can bust this right into my bedroom, but instead I simply say "Cool, follow me".

He was right, tonight is an exceptionally beautiful night. Although you can hear the downtown Atlanta street symphony it blends well with our outdoor dining. This dinner is excellent. Edward made steaks smothered in fresh sautéed spinach, onions and mushrooms and topped off with melted bleu cheese crumbles. The sweet potatoes were cooked to perfection and draped in a heavenly, almost sinfully concoction of brown sugar, honey butter and a brandy sauce. I thought I had died and woke up in "Food Network". "Why aren't you in someone's kitchen somewhere Edward, this is literally the BEST food I have ever tasted. You could be the head chef at a five star restaurant. Have you ever considered that" I asked. All he could do was blush and nod his head in appreciation. "I never really gave it much thought. My mother raised me to be able to fend for myself. I found the time to be up under her in the kitchen" he replied. "I knew you were a mama's boy...I bet you even know how to sew" I laughed. His lack of response and casual expression told me that I had hit the nail on the head. "Are you serious, you can cook and sew? You really don't need a woman, hell, you are one" I joked. He almost choked on this food after I said it from laughing so hard. "I mean really...you're the perfect wife. If we were to get together this would almost work. I'd bring home the bacon and you'd turn it into something amazing. I continued. "So, what is your ideal woman Mr. Sparks" I started with my next line of questioning. "I believe that it's my turn and you have yet to answer my last question ma'am" he reminded me. "Touché pussycat, well in MY opinion, I have always been a GREAT kisser. My very first book was actually *"Karen Kepplewhite is the World's Best Kisser"*. Since that moment, I kind of made kissing "my thing". It was my mission to literally take the souls of each person I kissed" we both laughed. "Seriously, I could tell when I walked away with another soul. It used to be so much fun, turning boys out, until I learned that what I was doing could eventually be harmful. But to answer your question, I would say I was an eleven in the KISS category. As far as sex goes...I think I'm average, I know that's like shooting myself in the foot since we haven't even gone there. It doesn't really give you much to look forward to". "So why do you say that, that you're average" he asked. "I don't want you to look at me funny or think that I'm being stuck up or anything...BUT...since the beginning of time, no really, since I started having sex, it seemed like the people that I was with were just so happy to BE there that they didn't require anything of me. All of my friends were getting thrown around and flipped through the air, while every guy I was with wanted to actually look me dead in my face while we did it. Like I was going to slip out on them or some shit, it was crazy. They didn't require different positions and dared not ask for head; and more than likely it was over as soon as it got started. The whole thing is that I know deep down that there is a sensual temptress just bursting at the seams waiting for someone to unleash her". "But who knows, I may just be all talk...wouldn't bust a grape. At an early age I made the decision then to NOT give second chances "sexually". I mean really, if you're going to show up I expect you to show out".

"Dang, why not give the brothers a break. They may have been stressing all day about what's going to finally go down" he said laughing jokingly. "Well he should have got that first one out before he got there. That way, I would be his round two or second wind". Edward placed his plate on the table and stood up. I was semi-nervous thinking that I had gone and done it again...stuck my foot in my mouth. "Where are you going" I asked perplexed. "To the bathroom to get this first round over with" he laughed. He kneeled down in front of me removing my plate from my lap and placing it on the table. "My turn" he said as he pulled my body towards him so quickly that I had thought hours had passed. Here we are again, so close that it feels like we are sharing the same breath. "Since you have decided to take a chance on me still being a work in progress, I would like to help you with your little problem, if you'd let me of course" he whispered. "What little problem are you referring to because I don't remember saying that I had any problems" I responded. We were so close right now that our lips mistakenly (*yeah right*) brushed up against one another. "Maybe you'll let me help you find that lost temptress inside of you" he said as he searched in my eyes for the answer. There is something about this man that makes me feel vulnerable and I do not like that feeling. When he's around me I feel inadequate or emotionally impotent. Maybe it's because I'm so use to always being in control. Maybe it's because I don't know anything about him. Maybe I'm doing what I've become best known for when meeting new prospects as I approach the possibilities of a new relationship and that's sabotage. For some reason unbeknownst to me, I'll either find or create a reason to get out of there. When I start feeling some type of way or I'm unable to locate any major flaws in the guy I have to call in the recon team to get me out of that situation. God forbid that I actually open up and give someone a chance. Do you want to know why? Because that same chance will eventually be thrown up in my face once they start to lie, cheat and steal. I don't mean like actually "stealing" (*although I did have one slimy son of a bitch take $60.00 out of my purse...this was before I was financially set. So that $60.00 might as well have been $6000.00*). The "stealing" of an individual's time is what I'm referring to, because as you can see, I got back that $60.00 (*and then some*), but I will never be able to get back those seconds, minutes, hours, days, months and years.

There should be a law against people "stealing" people's time. But then again, if they put that law into action someone will more than likely want restitution for broken hearts and if that ever happens then I'd be looking at a life sentence. Fuck it...I'll just cut my losses and call it a "Learning Experience", and as *Miki Howard* said it "Experience is a good teacher".

When I return from my daydream I find Edward still looking at me with his hands resting on my thighs. I feel uneasy because I can't remember if I was supposed to be answering a question or if I was the last one talking. I guess I'll just sit here and look foolish until he gets the hint to repeat himself. I don't have to wait long before he starts talking and catches me back up to where we had left off.

"Erica I've never met anyone like you and trust me I've met plenty of women. It's just something about you. You give off this persona that you are so tough and that you can do everything for yourself, like you don't need anyone. But I think that's false, I think underneath that façade you're as fragile as a butterfly's wings. I want to be the person that you undress for emotionally. I don't want you to have to carry the weight of the world on your shoulders. I want you to know that there are people out there who are strong enough to carry you; you and all of your dreams and more importantly all of your fears. I may not be the man at the end of your story, but I'd love to help rewrite some of these chapters.

IN A PERFECT WORLD

List what you will **_NOT_** deal with in a relationship or mate **(DON'T BEND):**

_____

_____

_____

_____

_____

_____

_____

_____

_____

_____

_____

_____

_____

_____

_____

_____

_____

_____

List what you **_WANT_** in your relationship or next/current mate:

_____

_____

_____

_____

_____

_____

_____

_____

_____

_____

_____

_____

_____

_____

_____

_____

_____

_____

Chapter Four

"Only as faithful as his/her Options"

I think it is quite apparent that my "trust-o-meter" needs a tune-up. Well, when you've been single for as long as I have you tend to do whatever you can do to NOT fall for the old okie-doke. I truly believe that if I would have remained programmed in my initial state *(of confusion)* I would be in the same situation that most women find themselves in today. I often tell men upon meeting them that I am NOT like most women you've met or will ever meet in your lifetime. I'm not saying that "I'm better" or more unique, it's just a fair warning that you may have met your match. I think it's only fair since the surgeon general failed to attach the WARNING label for the general consumer (*dater*). I'm not sure why but it appears that the powers that be supplied me with a bit more testosterone than other women. So needless to say, I don't cry at weddings or feel some type of way when friends are gushing over their new bundles of joy. GREAT...you've created a *"person"*. I'm sure you'll find both happiness and sorrow in that decision. Don't get me wrong, they're cool, it's just NOT for me. I don't believe in creating drama where there is none. I like being able to get up and go much too much to have to start getting in the habit to see if I've left anyone behind. I haven't gotten past my selfish phase and I'm not sure when I will so I refuse to bring anyone into a situation where I am not willing to give *"all of me"*; which explains WHY I refuse to get into a committed relationship. When my grandmother planted the seed that *"Men are only as faithful as their options"* I had no idea at the time that women could be just as guilty of that as well, if not more so at times. Although many of us would hate to admit to it, facts are facts. Just like men we have the ability to say *"yes or no"* to that innocent lunch date or the *"No strings attached"* flowers, candy or fruit basket. Often with women it begins with the simple *"you look so beautiful today"* compliments that our counterparts failed to give us that morning. Not to mention men's go to line to spark a conversation and gain more information. You know the line, *"tell your husband that he is one lucky man"*. That's when we are supposed to come back with *"I'm not married or I'm actually single"*.

Speaking of lunch, I have about three people that I need to confirm or decline for this week. I'm not a player...I just "lunch" a lot, LOL. *"Brian"* is a guy I met through a mutual friend. The first person that I have

ever dealt with outside of my color guidelines. He's a

professional guy who stands at a comfortable 6' even,

which means that I can wear my heels with him. One

of the biggest things that bother me with him is that

he clearly shops off the *"rack"*. Meaning that

whatever the mannequin is wearing is how he takes it.

No sort of style or swag, he's just *"there"*. I feel like his

mother each time we go out, *"Are you sure you want*

to wear that...outside...in public...where people can see

you" I find myself saying the same thing over and over

again; often times like *"mother's"* do. I have been

avoiding sex at all cost. I honestly don't believe that it

has anything to do with HIM, it's all psychologically

unstable me. I just have this false illusion that white

people are *"mushy"* to the touch. I know it sounds

bazaar, but it's MY truth. I just have an image in my

mind of my fingers sinking into their skin when I touch them, so that completely destroys the video image playing in my mind when it comes to SEX. I swear to goodness, I'm so damn petty! Just call me "*Petty Labelle, Petty by Nature, Petty Murphy...Petty or Not, Here I Come*". I'm an asshole, but then again, I never claimed to NOT be one. Thinking about him has caused me to pull my phone out to text him, just in order to bring his thoughts of Erica to the forefront of his frontal lobe. He's not a bad conversationalist either; I just have to stay abreast of every current event that is of any importance. I swear it seems like he's more for Human Rights and the entire **#BlackLivesMatter** movement than I am...and I'm the black person here. I mean, black folks are "*straight*" but geesh, he's like a white Martin Luther King. No really, I'm down for the cause but I don't think I'm going to be marching anywhere...bad back...bad knees

(*you understand*). Brain makes sure that I never want

for anything. He's my mister *"Fix-it"*, but not the

handyman type, he does however have the bank

account to call on said handyman. All I have to do is fix

my lips to say that something in my life is amiss. Brian

is the kind of gentleman who you never have to ASK

for something. I don't care if it's the same thing he got

me LAST month just in a different color, he's on it

without constant reminders and dropping hints. There

have been many times that I've called in or logged

online to pay a bill and it has already been

paid...THAT'S WHAT I'M TALKING ABOUT! In return I

make him look like the man in front of his business

partners, and lowest of keys, I'm sure that women

silently flock to him when they see how *"well-kept"* he

keeps me. I am his real life Cinderella or American Girl doll. I just make him look better…and feel better.

Now about that check-in:

TEXT FROM ME: Hey there handsome, how are you today? Have you been thinking about me?

Not even a full minute has gone by…

TEXT FROM BRIAN: BROWN SUGAR!! I'm doing great, how about you? You entered my dream last night…did I happen to show up in yours?

Now, here is where I can tell a full blow LIE or a small "untruth" just to allow him to save face; OR I could just give it to him STRAIGHT…NO CHASER!

TEXT FROM ME: DREAM…you have to SLEEP in order to dream (*right*)? I wish I could say that you did but I have not been getting any sleep these days.

TEXT FROM BRIAN: Aww, baby that's why you need me to take you away for a while. Let me spoil you, maybe get that sexy body of yours in a nice string bikini while we lay on the beach of someone's island. What do you think about that?

Okay HERE is where it gets TRICKY! I mean, I would LOVE to go and frolic on a beautiful island, I just don't want to go with HIM. All that mushy, pale, un-sculpted skin glaring in the suns magnificent light...uh, nope!

TEXT FROM ME: You are hands down the sweetest man that I have ever met. You should come with a warning from the surgeon General that you may give TOOTH ACHES. So sweet you're going to give me a cavity (*this is where I'd insert the winking emoji just for good measure*). I will let you know as soon as my calendar clears up some. *"Love waits for no man"* so my job is never done here. Thank you for thinking of me. Until we get our island vacation I hope this will suffice...

The attachment I send him caters to the male libido but still leaves much to the imagination. This should hold him over for another couple of months. You see, men don't require as much as women think. They are VERY simple creatures. Often times even simpler than their BEST FRIENDS...the DOG!

- Feed him

- Walk him

- Play with him

- Caress his belly (*or more*)

- Reward him for good behavior

It is actually THAT simple. After you've done everything that YOU were supposed to do, if he still wants to hop his ass off the porch and go play with the other dogs, then it is what it is. As long as he

doesn't bring you back any FLEAS *(Females Lurking*

Everywhere And Shit), then we are good here. When

you really think about it, most people only want to be

bothered when they want to be bothered anyway.

Why not come up with a schedule and take some of

the stress off yourself? I kinda like my Monday's to

digress and reflect on the week ahead...see you on

HUMP DAY my dude! I leave my white boy alone on

that note and move on to my email. I try to relay to

every friend on a different platform (*to not get folks*

and conversations mixed up). As all lessons I learned

this the HARD way when I mistakenly sent a reply text

to my sister talking about another person...but failed

to disengage the original conversation, and in true

Erica Brown form I gave this girl the business. I talked

about everything from the muskrat that sat atop her

dome to the deformity of her right foot. I mean how many people do YOU know that have ALL pinky toes on one foot. I went in too, no holds barred. I think I said something about *"Not being able to complete an entire nursery rhyme on one-foot ass girl"*. Yeah, can't really talk your way up out of that one...but don't think for one moment that I didn't try. It's through all of these trial and error periods throughout my life that makes it possible for me to help others. I did all of this for YOU; or at least that's what I've always tried to convince myself. That's easier to digest than to admit that I'm just a super bitch. A hateful being who is the reason that this particular *"nameless"* individual only wears closed toe shoes 365 days a year. Before, she would let the *"Pinky Piggy's"* out of the pin.

STUPID SMART PHONE!!!

Oh well, you live and you learn. I like to think that that mis-text helped in a way. If not for her, then for onlookers.

Back to people being ONLY as faithful as their OPTIONS...it's true you know. I have a very dear friend named Kelli **@queenkells718** who makes it her business to search the "world wide web" whenever she meets a new person. I've never seen anything like it before. I'm the kind of person that if you send me a Friend Request on social media, I'm accepting. NOT Kelli, baby, she turns up the brightness on the computer and even talks to the screen. I was in the office with her one day when a new request came thru and it was GAME ON! She enlarged the picture and after studying it for a minute she moved on to mutual friends. Lord forbid they had "NO MUTUAL FRIENDS", she was like *"Oh hell no, who sent you"*? I always wanted to ask her what if *"just maybe"* the

person came across your profile and decided *"hey, I'd*

like to know more about this person". After being

around her I have to say that it rubbed off on me a

little. I started looking at people with the side eye

wondering *"who sent you"*, which is not always a good

thing especially since I have my social media accounts

strictly for networking purposes, so I need to be

accepting every lonely heart that slides in my DM

(*direct message...for all of my old heads*).

Like clockwork my little Oriental connection *"Dave"*

makes sure to send me my *"daily"* good morning

email. He is such a sweetheart, always sending poetry

and virtual flowers. Not a day goes by that he doesn't

send me an inspirational and/or motivational quote,

followed up by some freaky meme; which I guess

makes him a *"Spicy Eggroll"*. Oh, if you haven't caught

on by now, Dave is Asian...but he has a white name

and he acts *"black"*. I tell you the boy is all kinds of

mixed up, but I adore his sweet spirit. He's the man I

turn to when I just need someone to listen. He doesn't

know it, but he will NEVER escape the friend zone

(*bless his heart*). I'm sure you've heard people claim

that a person is just *"too nice"*, well it's a very true

statement; especially if you yourself are a more

complex person with undiagnosed multiple

personality disorder. I mean honestly, who wants to

stand in a field full of lilies and sunflowers while

butterflies flutter overhead and hummingbirds sing

the same friggin song over and over and over again. I

just picture the person sitting across from you dressed

in khakis and a plaid button up shirt in competition

with the red and white checkerboard picnic blanket

and (*although I don't personally have one...but always*

wanted one) a wicker picnic basket that's holding the blanket down while a soft wind circles you as love floats in the air. Uh, nobody, that's damn who...not all of the damn time. Sometimes you want Timberland's and a wife beater (*the tank top, not some dude known for knocking bitches out*), but a man that lets you know that he is THERE! Save all of that soft spoken nonsense for someone else, whispering all the damn time like we are constantly in a library or something. Show me something that I've never seen before. Take me somewhere I've never been. Make me feel something other than what YOU think is the be all to end all in YOUR grand scheme of things. Yes, I'm talking about the penis. I hate to break it to most of you men...but you aren't "*killing*" us. Most women are BORN actors (*or actresses, for our politically correct people*) or thespians to those who understand. I guarantee that I have someone reading right now saying "*I think she spelled lesbian wrong*".

Back to what I was saying, you may hit a "*spot*" but 97% of you quickly disengage once you see a change of expression or increase in volume. If only you understood to just "*keep doing what you're doing*" don't add that extra swirl because YOU think you can up the ante on the feeling-o-meter. Seriously, in all honesty, you could have left that extra horizontal dance move at home Mr. Jabbawockee, this ain't "*Dancing with the Stars*" or "*So You Think You Can Dance*".

I will be the first to say that I firmly agree that feelings or true love makes "*sex*" that much better, but let's be real here, every time you lay down for a roll in the hay you don't want to lay down with "*Mr. Nice Guy*". I'll say it, sometimes **NICE** gets boring. It's a FACT that both MEN and WOMEN cheat and it's just as simple as that. Before you jump down my throat, I DID NOT SAY EVERYONE; but the percentage is NOT low. How can I be so sure you ask? It's simple, in today's world the definition of cheating has become so murky and broad. It is not just a physical act anymore. At one point in time you would have to actually swap bodily fluids for it to be considered *"cheating"*. Nowadays all you have to do is *"Like"* another person's picture or follow them on social media. If you want to get biblical all you have to do is THINK about another person and you've already crossed the line. For real? You can't even THINK about another person without being accused of cheating? Sometimes it takes cutting the person's head off that's beneath you and sewing on *"Larenz Tate, David Beckham or Dewayne Johnson's"* head just to reach the point of climax and it's not because we don't love you or we're not attracted to you anymore. It can be as simple as you have pissed us off so much that the very thought of you turns our stomach; which we know will soon pass, but for right NOW...go play in traffic, in the HOV lane! Just because your significant other is in your presence doesn't mean that he/she is there in mind, body and spirit. I think that *"Jennifer Lewis"* said it best in the movie *"Not Easily Broken"* "When they STAY and they done already LEFT...they get MEAN" and with this you can use the word "mean" however you want. You can use it in the physical sense or in the emotional sense, because if/when a person really loves you, how can they live with themselves knowing that THEY are the cause of your tears and heartache. It just doesn't add up. Think about it.

Dave wants to have dinner tonight and although the thought of a FREE MEAL rings like my favorite song in my head...I just don't feel like being bothered or entertaining one of these *"Lord take me NOW"* boring ass NICE men tonight. He's a sweetheart but I need a bit more of a challenge this evening. Oddly enough my mind keeps floating back to *"Mr. Can Claim You on My Taxes"*. There is something so intriguing about him, a mystery that is keeping him on my mind. He's nowhere around but I can smell his cologne and that feeling begins to rise up inside of me again. I think I will call him (*remember, Brian is text and Dave is email*), I have a guy who I only deal with through the US Postal Service or snail mail. His name is Roger and I can honestly tell you that if he resided within my same postal code I would adopt the popular slogan from the television show *"Sister Sister"* (*with those twins Tia* and Tamera Mowry)*; when the little boy from the group "IMX" (*Marques Houston*) would come over unannounced to proclaim his undying love for the BOTH of them: "Go home Roger, Go home Roger...GO HOME, GO HOME, GO HOME"!!!

See, Roger had the right idea, why settle for one when you can have them both. Don't worry this is NOT the advice that I give my clients, but I do share it with family and friends. I have tried to bring my older sister Melanie over to the dark side with me but she will be a hopeless romantic until the day she dies, unless she dies from a broken heart before that. I mean she is the type of bleeding heart who believes in true love and she has always been under the unfortunate delusion that she can actually *"change"* a person. The ONLY time that you can change another person is when they are in diapers. She is the true reason behind how and why I developed my highly popular relationship kit "**You've Got Love**". I have seen her broken down by love one hundred too many times and I wanted to try and develop something that could change that for her and other sappy souls just like her. Which reminds me, I need to call her. We haven't spoken in a minute. Not that anything happened to create a gulf between us or anything, it's just that "Life Happens" and when it does sometimes old habits and routines just don't make their way on your schedule. Although 24 hours sounds like ample time to do everything, it just doesn't work out like that.

The phone rings about four times before Melanie finally answers, our normal sibling lyrical exchange begins: "I don't know why you don't say hello when you answer" I said. Melanie quickly retorted by saying "Bitch, when you don't hear it ringing anymore and don't get the greeting, you know that it's me". "It

could be any damn body asshole. I don't know if it's

that piece of a man that you have or my sweet niece.

How is she doing anyway? I normally hear from her by

now" I said. She told me that she was at her acting

classes. The girl swears that she's going to be the next

big thing. You wouldn't know that you were talking to

a little child if you closed your eyes listening to the

things she says. She thinks she's grown, but she will

always and forever be my baby. She's my mini me

since I don't have any of my own and I refuse to get a

pet. "So, what are you doing right now, wanna go grab

something to eat" Melanie easily slid in. Although

Melanie is beyond financially capable of taking care of

herself I pick up the bill every chance I get. During my

darkest times (*and there were many*) she was always

there, supportive in every way possible. We are closer

than any siblings walking the face of this earth. The kind of sisters who would take a rubber bullet for each other...LOL. I told her yes and we decided to meet at the local TGI Friday's out near Stone Crest Mall in Lithonia, GA. "Don't be trying to over dress either Erica, I don't feel like having to pull things together just to damn eat, it's not that serious" Melanie snorted. I know that she's the big sister but the seniority is just not there to accept this tone. She's lucky I like her a little bit. "I was just going to throw on anything because it honestly just feels like one of those days" I said. "Oh hell, let me see if I threw away my old prom dress. I might even have a few bridesmaid dresses hanging around" Melanie said as she laughed. It was good to hear her laugh again, because it had been so long. She is good for allowing someone to steal her smile and with as many teeth that she has, when it's gone it feels like someone took the sun away. "Do you need to be picked up since I know that you're allergic to driving" she said; "And you forgot to mention that traffic makes my ass itch" I added. "No actually, I'm fine, I will meet you there around one o'clock. That will give me enough time to meet with my client and finish up some other work that's been staring at me for the past three days. Gives us just enough time to get some drinks in before lunch" I stated. "Cool, I will see you there. I'll be the one in the wedding dress" she laughed. "Well just make sure that it's not a white dress because that would be false advertisement hooker" I laughed and hung up before she could even muster up a snappy comeback. Now I have to pick something out to wear that will piss her off.

****

I intentionally arrive twelve minutes and fifty-three seconds late because I know that it pisses Ms. Corporate America completely and absolutely off. I can't even hide my giddiness when I enter Friday's. Melanie tries her best to hide her irritation but I know her too damn well. I can't even sit down before the chastising begins. "Why in Jesus Christ do you always have to be late" she scolded me. "Well hello to you too doll face" I say as I hand her a beautifully wrapped, for no good reason at all, except the fact that she is a phenomenal sister and dictator. "This little tiny bullshit is not about to change the fact that I'm sick of you leaving me waiting for you" Melanie retorted. She haphazardly opened the package and pulled out a beautiful diamond encrusted purse hanger. She had admired the one I had so much the last time that we had dinner that I had to make sure that she got one of her own. As you see, I love my sisters' big eared self...LOL! I bet she can hear me right now.

"So what's new in the interesting land of the black Erica Kane" Melanie said. She's been calling me Erica Kane ever since our mother used to force us to watch the soaps with her. Well actually it started off as forced but after a while the people on the small boob tube became family. We laughed when they laughed and hurt when they hurt and God forbid if someone DIED on the stories! What in the hell am I going to do without my Uncle Luke and Aunt Laura?

I actually already know what I'm ordering so I'm just looking through this menu out of habit. I'm a creature of habit and when it comes to food, I'm not really interested in change. Melanie sees that I'm ignoring her little Erica Kane nod so she continues to push.

"You'll never believe who I saw over the weekend. I tried to call you but I didn't have any reception". Melanie didn't even wait for my response before she continued to talk. "Well remember when we were in high school out in Roswell"? "Where pray tell are you talking about Crestwood or Chattahoochee High. We've attended a number of institutions of education in our day" I slid in using my best southern bell accent. She thought for a second before she finished "Shit, I don't even know. But it doesn't matter because he didn't even go to our school. Remember he was a sexy ass chocolate thang. This shouldn't be that difficult since there were only a handful of black folks that we knew in that sea of white folks and even less when you talk about the ones that you would actually like to talk to" she said. She was right it only took a second to figure out that she was talking about Aaron. Back then he was a tall and slender, artificial hair wearing, singing like a song bird chocolate God. During that time in my life my level of voyeurism was confined to watching guys that I didn't necessarily think would ever give me the time of day. For some reason my self-esteem was super low and I never quite felt like I was good enough for people. Most of the time I equated perfection with intelligence. I said it then and I will say it again, I am NOT smart, I am creative, and there is a BIG difference. My sister Melanie is smart; I am great at manipulating the situation to ensure that things work in my favor. My father told me growing up that I was a "Con" but before I could take it as an insult he explained to me that being a "Con" was not necessarily a bad thing. He said that being a con only meant that I have the ability to "Convince" people to do things. Ultimately the decision is yours, I am just merely making a suggestion or offering an alternative solution that you may have possibly overlooked. I didn't find out until years later that the guy Aaron that I admired from a distance actually held the same feelings. I would have never guessed in a million years that this perfect creature who was crooning millions would be any kind of "shy" when it came to interacting with certain females. I learned all of this when our paths crossed again as adults. It was probably best because I was kind of out there as a teenager. In one of my "finding myself" moments I joined a girl group which was completely crazy since I've honestly never in my life wanted to even sing. I only sang because I was expected to. I made the final decision to never sing again after I was offered a million-dollar contract from Motown Records and my group members completely stopped speaking to me during that negotiation period. It wasn't until I

declined the offer that my sister and bestie retrieved

their voices that were lost during that entire

week...it's funny how things work out, huh. I never

thought walking into this stranger's apartment that

night for vocal lessons would reveal a ghost from my

past. I believe that I was born to be late so even then

my punctuality was nonexistence so needless to say I

was the last to arrive to rehearsal. When I walked in

the room I could already feel the dread rising for

making the decision to join this singing group, why

didn't I just say NO? That all changed when he walked

from the other room. The others knew immediately

that there was a connection but they had no idea that

there was a past. Although I was a much more mature

and confident woman then there are just some people

who just have the ability to take your breath away and

replace your confidence with silly putty. I'm not sure

how long I had checked out but when I returned I was

in his arms. However; these weren't the same arms

these arms were sculpted and strong, with abs and

more to match. It was like something out of a dream.

For so long he had been the object of perfection, my

scale for comparison when I met other men. My

dream guy was twirling me around like someone in

one of those Caucasian romance movies. He was still

beautiful and the body was to die for. Once my feet

returned to earth and my mind shortly followed I was

now face to face to the man of my dreams, but as I

stated I was a completely different Erica now. This

reaction sort of threw me for a loop because all I

could remember from years ago was eyeballing him

from across the room or the occasional awkward

hello. This long lost friendship hug had me thinking

that maybe he actually remembered showing up in my dreams every night...that's honestly the only way to explain it. I don't know how I made it thru that rehearsal because the only thing on my mind was how he would feel inside me. One day during a scheduled rehearsal it appeared that I was the ONLY group member who didn't receive the cancellation text and showed up at his door (*that wasn't nothing but the Lord*). After he realized that my cluelessness was genuine he laughed and invited me in. I tried to decline but he made the point that I was there now so I might as well come on in for a few minutes. Needless to say that those minutes turned into hours and by the time I looked up it honestly made no sense to even go home. Aaron offered me a t-shirt and his bed with no strings attached while he took the couch. From different rooms, while we were supposed to be going to sleep we continued to talk about our lives and what we thought was missing. We hinted about our desires but never once divulged that they included each other. You could feel the passion in every single pause. To this day I never understood why the new me and the new him didn't bridge that gap and fulfill that lustful desire. The conversation had reached a point of such extreme and passionate lust that it caused me to return his shirt and tell him that I had to go (*that wasn't nothing but the Devil*). Aaron begged for me to stay stating that I was tired and it was late and he wouldn't be able to sleep until I made it home safely. Even as I recount that night I can feel my blood pressure rising. My heart is beating faster than my fingers can type (*ignore the fact that I'm probably the world's slowest typer...you catch my drift*).

SIDEBAR: Is anyone else fucking hot right now or is that just me?

Okay, where were we. Little did he know that I was mentally already in bed with him...I had to get out of there.

"Baby girl don't leave. Is it something that I said, am I making you feel uncomfortable? I promise we can stop talking and just go to sleep" he said. For some reason I felt a lump growing in my throat, larger than the lump growing in my stomach. I honestly felt like I would explode if I didn't get out of there. I was so sexually destructive at that time that the last thing I wanted Aaron to be was another notch on my headboard, he was so much more to me than that, but I was still not ready to admit that to him or myself for some reason. It wasn't until about five years later that our paths led us to the bedroom and dear God when I tell you that this man made love to every square inch of my body, not to leave out my soul. The care and attention that he paid to the prime real estate lying beneath him was something out of a dream. Like literally everything about this man is perfect. If he had been an artist, then I was his canvas and with every single stroke we created a masterpiece. I don't think that I mentioned that he was a major recording artist. That night every aspect of his performance was award winning. His voice rang in my ear and was as equally erotic and mesmerizing as each stroke. Have you ever been with someone where your bodies fit together so perfectly that you're sure that your real names had to be Adam and Eve? From lying in his arms to him connecting his plug into my matrix was nothing short of paradise. It sounds crazy now to say that I felt a spiritual connection with him, but then again I supposed the Devil is in the

spiritual realm of things. It always concerned me that

he never completely appeared to be available. I'm not

saying that he didn't make me feel like I was the only

person in the world when I was with him, it's just that

something always seemed a bit off. It wasn't until

later that I found out that he had been in a

relationship each and every time that our paths

crossed. Allow me to add "magician" as another one

of his many talents. When you disappeared as often

as this man did, you had to be a Master Magician. I

guess I was just the lucky girl he picked to be the

magicians' assistant. It was just all smoke and mirrors

when he would pull that rabbit out of his hat…I was all

his. Hook, line and sinker. WHY…ARE YOU FUCKING

SERIOUS? Why not just be 100 with folks? You never

know what a person is willing to do when given the

opportunity to decide on their own. That was another nudge to make the old saying true that "A man is only as faithful as his options". I mean this man has proclaimed his undying love for me over the years and has always been attached at the hip to someone else. Whelp, there goes another one down the drain along with my ability to trust anyone with a pulse.

I just looked at Melanie unmoved. I was hoping that my "don't really give two damns" look would be enough to change the subject, but it wasn't. "No ma'am, this is not the reaction that I was looking for. What's the deal, you would normally need a diaper on every time I mention his name. What happened" she said. "Nothing, let's just say that I grew wiser and recognized my worth". I guess after a while you get tired of playing second fiddle to other women as well as their careers. Sometimes you just want to be priority" and with that said I was done with that topic.

We ordered our food and moved onto the next

subject which included chastising me for not settling

down. "You know this not trusting folks is growing

pretty old. You'll never find someone you trust 100%

Erica" Melanie said. "Especially when I'm not damn

looking Melanie" I interrupted her; saying my damn

name like she's my mama!

"I'm being serious, you are going to watch your entire

life slip by helping other people find and keep love

while you're secretly a love saboteur. How can you

preach something that you are completely against"

she questioned. "I'm not against love, I just know that

it's not for me" I replied. But this time I felt differently

when I said it. It almost felt like I was supposed to add

"right now" at the end. What was happening to me? I

feel like I'm turning into a sap or a punk. I don't like it...at all.

"What about the nice guy that you met a few months ago at the airport, he seemed really nice" Melanie quizzed. "He was nice, for someone else. He was handsome, supportive and such a gentleman. I found out shortly after meeting him that he was just an all-around team player when I ran into him Pride weekend" I said. "Bitch, no" Melanie gasped as she refused to believe it. "Bitch, yes" I said. "So how the hell do you know he was down there scouting for potential ass, no pun intended? You were there too and you aren't gay" she challenged. "I was there in my company shirt as a corporate sponsor. I didn't have on a hot pink baby tee that read "OPEN 24/7, Please Use the Back Door" I added and as quickly as that conversation started it ended. "I wish that I could change your outlook on men E" Melanie said with a

sigh. "My outlook will change as soon as men do. See,

your problem is that you have always believed that

you have the ability to change men. The only time you

can change a man is when they are in diapers and

even then you aren't really feeling their shit" I said.

"Well, all I'm saying is that men are not the only

beings who are not faithful, women can be some

sneaky and conniving people too, she replied. "I'm

sorry, just for clarification, you wouldn't be referring

to me by any chance, are you, because everyone that I

meet are fully aware that we are not exclusive. I don't

promise exclusivity to anyone. I allow each individual

the opportunity to decide their level of participation

in my life but I always let them know what I AM and

what I AM NOT looking for.

My like life (*because ain't no mo' love...inside joke*) is pretty much like a game of "tag", when it's your turn "you're it", simple as that. When I'm with someone I am completely attentive to their needs and hopefully I am everything that they need in that moment. I believe that if I'm NOT then I'm either NOT doing my job or I'm just not the person for you, and I'm okay with that. I'm a big enough girl to know that I'm not going to be everyone's dream girl per say" I said. "Honestly, what I hear you saying is that you're no better than them and you should change it to People are only as faithful as their options" said Melanie and in all honesty, she had a point. "I guess you're right, the only difference is that many men refuse to be completely transparent when dealing with women. I don't lead men on, I let people know from Jump Street what it is. I make no promises to anyone about anything, it's easier that way. You can't stop anyone

from cheating so why even try. All I ask is that you

don't disrespect me to my face" I ended the

conversation in a way that quietly said please change

the subject. "Check please" Melanie said quickly

waving our server over. I guess that was it,

conversation over...until next time.

Take a minute and write down YOUR top five

QUALITIES and the top five you want in a mate!

Chapter Five

"Speed Dating"

I never come to silly stuff like this but I promised a few of my friends that I would try it out with them since it's like the thing to do right now. It also worked out that it was so close to home. I never knew that the coffee shop held these types of events. This just adds more reason to why this is my favorite little coffee shop. Maybe I will meet my "Cup of Joe" tonight. My roster isn't full yet.

I feel like bait in a sea full of lonely and desperate middle aged men. The shine coming from the tops of their domes is causing a migraine. Don't get me wrong, I absolutely love a bald head. But don't you dare walk up to me with a sunroof in your afro. Boy Bye! Either come to terms with reality and let the top back and all of the windows down, then maybe we can have a conversation…maybe. During the ice breaker event we were adorned with these corny "Hello My Name Is" stickers so that people could remember the name of the cattle roaming the cafe. The first guy that sits down looks like his mother dressed him and I'm automatically irritated looking at this Easter Sunday clip on tie. I've summed up the fact that you still live with your mom and she continues to do your laundry…nope, NEXT!

LONELY GUY #1: Hello there sunshine…the names Charlie Brown.

I look at my name tag to see if I spelled Erica incorrectly…I didn't.

ME: I don't do pet names Charlie Brown…

LONELY GUY #1: I understand, no worries. But if you'll indulge me for just one moment I can actually tell you the one reason that would make this the perfect connection if you decided to give me a chance. I could make your day girl!

ME: What's that?

LONELY GUY #1: You wouldn't even have to change your last name.

He winks believing that he just came up with the best pick up line the world had ever heard.

ME: Make my day you say? Well, Charlie would you like to hear my idea of a perfect day.

LONELY GUY #1: I sure would sunshine...sorry, Erica.

ME: It starts out on a beautiful day something like today. I awake to a gorgeous yellow sun glowing against a silky blue background. The birds are chirping while the neighborhood kids are running through plush green pastures. I roll over to you, gazing in your eyes, wearing the new skimpy red little teddy that I purchased with your credit card, that I know will turn you on. Then I reach under the cover and my hand running up your leg and...

Charlie is just about ready to fall out of his chair. Just as I'm about to get to the good part the bell rings.

ME: Oops, I guess there was a black out and now you have blue balls...sorry Charlie!

LONELY GUY #1: Wait...what?

NEXT

In a minute I'm about to get irritated and I haven't even been here that long. I see my girlfriend across the room and judging by the smirk on her face she's falling for the old razzle dazzle. That's what happens with people, yes people, not just women. When we meet people we already have this preconceived notion or image of what we think the perfect person is. For guys it is often a beautiful and humble lady, with a good head on her shoulders. One who doesn't really like to go out with her girls, loves to cook and clean and ready to drop his baby when he's ready. In an ideal world she's only been with one or two other guys sexually, unless of course she's the unicorn (*virgin*) that many guys are looking for. Boys are so stupid. This is not "Little House on the Prairie" and most girls aren't Laura Ingles. She will be a lady in public and a freak in private. She'll curve any other dude, including his friends, yes, it's true guys, your boys try to slide in the DM from time to time.

For her she might be looking for the image of what's been drilled into our mental rolodex since the beginning of time and that would be our knight in shining armor. He is a sharp dresser who loves God and treats his mother like a Queen WITHOUT being a freaking MAMA'SBOY, because there is a HUGE difference. His height will compliment her when she wants to put on her highest heels *(unless she really is open to no height restrictions to ride that ride)*. He will leave a scent behind that will dance around her nostrils all day. When it comes to other women he has complete and absolute tunnel vision. The deli special hanging in between is legs will keep her deep freezer stocked all spring, summer and winter long. He treats her like she is the prize and will do nothing to ever mess that up...and SCENE! I say scene because that is a fairytale scenario that will get your feelings hurt every time.

The next guy that slides into the open seat in front of me is handsome with his flawless skin and dimples that seem to be bottomless. Although he is fully clothed his muscular physique is pushing its way to the surface. Nice enough playground if I don't say so myself. I'm not sure of his nationality but I'd be confident to say that he isn't full blooded white American. The bell rings and the games begin. He politely reaches out to shake my hand and my question is answered when his heavy accent wraps around me...

LONELY GUY #2: Good evening, let me start by saying you look beautiful tonight.

ME: Thank you very much, the names Erica.

LONELY GUY #2: "I kinda picked up on that from the name tag but I appreciate the confirmation because you could have been Erica's representative".

ME: "I concur" I take a peek at his name tag "Nicholas". What brings you here tonight?"

LONELY GUY #2: "Uber"

ME: "Did you say Uber? Should I assume that's by choice or circumstance"?

LONELY GUY #2: "I did say Uber. It's most definitely by choice. I have a few toys to choose from but I'm just visiting for the week and it would have been impossible to drive. Besides I felt like drinking tonight so to play it safe I decided to Uber on down here, which by the way is a nifty little system you guys have. Since I know that you aren't here because you are having trouble finding a man, I'll assume that you are

the wingman to…"

He holds the letter o in "to" until I point out my

blushing friend from across the room.

ME: That pretty little thing across the room.

LONELY GUY #2: "Yes, Tabitha, right? We've met, she

seems like a really nice girl. Would you suggest that I

entertain that connection"?

I have to confess that I'm taken aback by his question

because I was under the assumption that he was here

to meet me.

ME: "I'm sorry, are you asking me if you should date

my friend instead of asking me what my favorite

restaurant is and what kind of flowers I like?"

LONELY GUY #2: "Indeed I am. Don't be offended, I'm

just not in the habit of banging my head up against a

brick wall. I left my helmet at home. You're gorgeous and if you were actually looking I would have my assistant schedule my private jet and take you to my favorite restaurant *"Le Chemise"* in Paris. But that would have been if you were available or at least interested".

The bell rings louder and more violently than before which causes me to jump.

LONELY GUY #2: I hope you find what you're heart desires Erica.

He kisses my hand and walks away. My eyes follow him but my mind is stuck on his last sentence. I'm in such a trance that I don't even notice when *"Mr. I'm Back"* sits in front of me. Not even the ringing of the bell breaks my trance. I don't even hear his voice, it wasn't until someone walks through the door which causes the breeze to make the fragrance travel from

his neck and smack me dead in the face. When I

return from my mental trip, sitting in front of me in a

white long sleeve collared shirt and brown apron is

the man, the myth, Edward Starks. It had been weeks

since I had seen him. I'm not sure what happened it

just seemed like time began to become null and void

and his calls and messages got lost in the shuffle. He

had sent me some more flowers but at the time the

larger more exotic bouquets from other suitors

seemed to over shadow his smaller attempt at getting

my attention. Not being a bitch, just stating the facts.

At the time I really wanted to send a mass email to all

of them that said "Try Edible Arrangements". Trust me

when I tell you, chocolate covered oranges and

caramel filled pretzels leave a much stronger impact in

a girl's book. I was almost at a loss for words when his

smile seemed to brighten the room. I almost got the feeling that I missed this man sitting in front of me who I still didn't know that well. I did know however that the short time that we did spend in each other's company was nothing short of amazing. Unfortunately, that same light that once lit the room turned into a spot light as it shined down on the stiff brown apron he was sporting. Before we could even utter a simple hello the third lonely guy of the evening tapped Edward on his shoulder and said, "Excuse me sir but I think you're in my seat and while you're at it bring me back a coffee, black with two sugars and no cream". At that point the only thing that Edward could say was "Yes sir, right away". There was something about this guy. He walked away not appearing to have been in any way offended by what just happened. He kept a pleasant disposition and just smiled as he scurried to retrieve this assholes order. I, however was pissed at how this person in front of me took the opportunity to bully someone who he obviously deemed beneath him. It enrages me to see people treat other people this way. Money doesn't make you magnificent or place you in a higher bracket than others. It just makes you a bigger assholes with more zeros.

LONELY GUY #3: "You can thank me later for saving you from the coffee boy".

He proceeded to laugh at his own whack attempt at stand-up. I quickly retorted by snapping,

ME: "No, allow me to thank you right now for showing me what kind of person you truly are because I would have never gotten back these three minutes that you were about to rob me of".

I stormed past Edward and out the front door. I'm not sure why that guy got under my skin so badly. I had the gut wrenching feeling that it was hitting too close to home for some reason. This isn't how I treat people...is it? No, that guy was an ass. I don't belittle people and look down on folks. I know how it feels to grow up with nothing and claw for dear life at each opportunity that presents itself until you make it.

But this wouldn't bother me so much if there weren't some actual truth to it. It might be time to reevaluate my own personal make-up.

We all have deep *Invention of a Man* dark relationship secrets **that we** keep hidden...what is your deepest darkest secret? Would it help you to EXPOSE it or would it hurt you?

_____

_____

_____

_____

_____

_____

_____

_____

_____

_____

_____

_____

Chapter Six

Building Mr. Right

I'm not sure why I agree to these things knowing full well that I am not the least bit interested. I haven't been back to the coffee shop for weeks. I honestly couldn't bear to see the look of embarrassment on Edward's face after what happened last time. The way that guy tore him down by hardly even saying anything would have been more than I could deal with. However, the difference between myself and Edward is the poisonous venom that drips from the tip of my tongue. I would have read that arrogant bastard from index to glossary using only a fourth graders spelling word list. That's how phenomenal I am with destructive words and cutting people up who deserve it. After looking around the café it appeared that Edward was off that night. I was happy but at the same time I was dying to catch a glimpse of him. Tonight is Melanie's birthday and I would have taken the chic anyplace in the world but she wanted to hit the comedy show at the coffee shop. I can't front, comedy is my "go to" for a great time. I didn't know they had comedy here on Thursday's but I'm glad I let her talk me out the house. With work and fighting with my own personal demons I had been held up in my loft for what felt like years and it was time to rejoin society. Because Melanie refused to do anything of substance for her birthday I was able to at least convince her to join me for a spa day where afterwards we went shopping for outfits for this evening. It's not like the dress code for the café was "dress to impress" but I make it my business to look red carpet ready wherever I go. However; tonight is Melanie's night.

Melanie was blessed with better locks than I and that is fine with me because I have a bigger butt. Yes, I'm being petty but you have to find your wins wherever you can. She decided on getting her hair rodded to follow its natural curl pattern anyway. All she really has to do was throw some water on that shit and she would have saved me $120.00 but like I said, it's her damn day. We didn't go to my girl Shanna this time, we went to "Super Cuts". Yeah, I said it "Super Cuts". Trust me, if you're of African American descent I can already see your face. I looked the same way the first time Melanie carried me up in there. I looked at her like "Bitch, I don't need no nine dollar blunt front, bowl cut hairstyle like I'm a damn third grade math teacher". If I'm lying, I'm flying. I sat in that chair and told that heffa "I better not get up out this damn chair

looking like Lloyd from Dumb and Dumber" and I

meant that shit! When I tell you that I fell in love with

a woman that day and her name is "Liza"

@liza.torres.186. Don't you hate watching your stylist

do something that appears to be so easy and get

home and try to reenact it and can't do it to save your

damn life? Liza does something with these damn flat

irons and then she gives it a little twirl with her finger

and viola...the PERFECT curl. Often times I don't even

recognize my own damn hair. Honestly, I bought the

exact same flat iron and all of the same products and

still, I got nothing. I'm starting to think it has nothing

to do with what she uses but instead it's that "finger"

of hers. I mean I too have a special finger...but I tend

to only use it for evil and not good. It normally helps

me when I'm driving. It changes purposes but that's

when I find it most useful. Other times it comes in handy for certain parts of my body, but I digress because I'm a lady.

The other thing Melanie has on me are these legs. I mean seriously, I bet when judgement day comes I'll learn that she took my portion which left me with the popsicle sticks that I try to keep covered up if I can help it. We found the perfect dress for her at a small boutique out near Phipps Plaza. I still question if it's really a shirt as appose to a dress as short as it is. But with legs like that you can pull off any lie. She loves her black clothes but I convinced her today to add some color to her funeral collection, and she did. The dress (*shirt*) was made of a soft yellow chiffon material. It had a strap going around the neck and a plunging bust. One side of the dress was completely open being held together with delicate buttons, while a long side train hung right above the floor. Maybe

that's where they're calling it a dress, but the rest of it

is barely covering her you know what...but that's none

of my business (*sips tea*). I actually purchased a few

dresses even though I already had in mind what I was

planning on wearing anyway. Some time ago my

elderly tailor, Ms. Mary, who finds her inspiration at

the bottom of a whisky bottle made me the sexiest

jumper that you've ever seen in your life. It's

sometimes difficult to feel sexy in something that's

covering 98% of your body but when I tell you that

this little number will bring a dead man back from the

grave...believe it! That lone 2% is from the neck to

where I was connected to my mother. It has huge

winged sleeves and fits just as perfectly as my skin.

The orange stretchy fabric clings to every dip and

curve on my body. There was no need to go

overboard with the accessories because the jumper was the headliner.

It wasn't until we arrived at the café that I saw that this was a dating comedy show. At this point I'm so sick of seeing desperately seeking people that I might go postal. Of course the only place to sit is the front near the makeshift stage. I don't care about getting talked about. I can take a joke and return one or two if you need to be taught a lesson. We sit at our little table and order some drinks from the mobile bar parked in front of the café. That is actually a really smart idea to get around having to obtain a liquor license. There were also a few food trucks out there to cover foods that weren't on the menu.

"Did your mother say what time she'd be here or is her plan to come in and be part of the show" Melanie said as she handed me my frozen Pina' Colada'. "I'm not sure. I haven't talked to her since we all left the spa. She knows what time the show starts and she's experienced the wrath before so I'm sure she will make it in more than enough time" I laughed as I remembered the last time she was casually late and comedian "Special K" **@specialk913** roasted her so hard that I thought they were going to bring out a platter and a shiny red apple to stuff in her mouth. He came over after the show to give her a hug and hit her with the "You know I was just joking mama" but by that time the damage had already been done. She retreated to her turtle shell for the remainder of the evening. It didn't stop Melanie and me from sticking our heads in her shell and burst into laughter drenched in tears. If it's funny, it's funny and that's the way the cookie crumbles.

Before we could really get into just how funny it was from across the room we see the old bird heading towards the table. "See, told you she ain't want no more" I said as we both laughed. A few minutes later the rest of the crew walked in fashionably late, but fashionable nonetheless. I see Denise **@mrsmarittaray** before anyone else standing at 6' 3" (*which she hardly ever admits to*). Right behind her is Tasha. She has always had the figure of a grown ass woman even in high school. If you look in the dictionary under "Bubble Butt" you're guaranteed to see that donk. These broads must have carpooled because giggling in the back bringing up the rear is Charmone, Brit and Mia. I refuse to hang with ugly chic's that would bring down my property value so the whole crew is a seven or better. I was wondering why the crowd looked so large and it's because all of these hoes brought dates. Now, I could have sworn that we had agreed NO DUDES tonight. Just as soon as I was about to say "at least Melanie and I know how to follow directions...her friend strolls in looking like he just left the set of the last "Cheech and Chong" movie *(higher than a kite)*. I'm done!! I can't stand when folks don't listen. I mean, I'm not tripping or anything, but damn. I could have asked someone to meet me here. Now I'm looking like the fifth wheel or damn driver. Normally I could count on our brother "Jay" to laugh with and talk about everyone in the room because no one is exempt when it comes to joaning folks. I bring out the absolute worst in my brother and that works out perfectly for me. Each time we are in tears when we link up, however, this fucker moved to Punta Cana on a whim. He didn't even tell us that he was moving until the week he was going and even that was an "of yeah, I'm moving to the DR". He may not be there all the time but he is most definitely there when we need him. As I lean over to converse with my mom I find an empty seat and her standing next to an older gentlemen under the threshold of the entrance. I'm not about to let these hussies ruin my evening, besides it's not my evening anyway. If Melanie is happy and from the look of her displaying every single tooth that she paid for...she is, and that's all that matters. The waitress stops by the table to clear away the trash and picks up the little slip that Melanie had filled out when we first sat down. I'm assuming they were little guest cards to add to the promoters email list. I just know she better had put down her own information. We often do that to each other as a joke.

I have to say that tonight's line up has been great. There were some cornballs that graced the stage but it wasn't too bad. Melanie and I pledged years ago to NOT laugh or even crack a smile if a comedian wasn't funny. We won't boo you, because that's rude, but we damn sure won't give you false hope when you should really be working at the Texaco on the corner. The host is one of our favorite comedians "Big Sean Larkins" **@sean_larkins** so we try to go support him whenever we can. Double D **@comediandoubled**, TK Kirkland **@tk_kirkland,** Big Kenny **@thebigkenny** and Tyler Craig are in rare form tonight as well. I can't get enough of his "And the Moral of the Story Is" jokes. Some comedians can get up there and say the same joke over and over again, as long as they change their shirt it's a new joke to me. After seeing the line-up it prompts me to believe that the café owner either has some serious money or some great contacts. Our

mom, Linda refuses to sit in the front with us anymore

so I get up to go check on her in between comedians.

She appears to be in good hands with her new friend.

He's a handsome chocolate man wearing a button

down shirt and some old man starched jeans. The kind

that stand in your closet instead of hang. He has a

head full of beautiful silver hair that I believe is his.

You can't tell anymore these days since men are just

as fake as women.

After I'm confident that she is okay I return to our

table. It appears that one of the crew paid for another

round of drinks. We toast to Melanie's birthday and

take the shots to the head. I'm not much of a drinker

anymore. I lost my taste for liquor when we were

around sixteen years old. The same crew with me

tonight were our road dogs growing up. We used to

spend the night at each other's house every single

weekend. It seemed like on the weekends when we

weren't with each other our separation anxiety would

set in to the point where our mothers would be like

"Get the hell out of my face and go find them damn

girls. Y'all act like you can't be away from each other

for two damn seconds" and they were right. One night

our mother came home (*early*) and found us with a

gallon of "Tanqueray" sniffing lines in her bedroom.

No, not cocaine, it was just corn starch. As I think back

we were some dumb asses. When Linda (*the old bird*)

walked in she went off! We tried to hide the bottle

but she snatched it from us and made us drink the

ENTIRE gallon and finish the lines of starch that we

had chopped up with the dull razor blade on her hand

mirror. She was sure to call all of the other girls

parents to give them a blow by blow (*no pun*

intended) of what we were doing and what she made us do. I never touched the "Green Monster" again. I didn't do too much hard drinking after that day.

One thing I can say is that there are quite a few good looking men in this place. Maybe they should have done name tags again today but this time add more information, like, what's their occupation. What's their marital status? I'm so over meeting men who are NOT married but their wives still are. I mean seriously how hard is it to just tell someone the damn truth? If you aren't happy anymore…say that! A persons feelings may be hurt but they'll live. It's when you waste a person's time; that is when it takes its toll. I refuse to believe that you can't find everything (*or close enough to it*) in one person. So you want me to believe that a man can't be handsome, sexy, successful, God fearing, respectful, ambitious, caring, sensitive, adventurous, passionate, seductive, romantic, responsible, funny and hung? So that man doesn't exist? But they say that God made man in his own image. So apparently God is some lying, cheating, ugly, baby bump stomach, irresponsible, little dick dog...is that it? Somebody needs to do their research then because I don't see that to be factual. The guys roaming the face of this earth must have a different daddy. God, you are NOT the father; Devil YOU are! Can you see God running off the stage in open toe shoes tripping over his white gown falling on the floor in the green room screaming "why"? The sad part is that God has no one to pray to, he's just simply stuck with these fucks. I can just see the camera pan back over to the Devil sitting their grinning looking evil, with his sculpted muscles glistening from the studio lights damn near blinding the audience. The glare almost shatters cameras one and two. Just sitting there knowing that he's won. Somebody get Maury on the phone.

I think if I had the choice of only five traits that I could pick to build my perfect man it would have to be:

- Fine- meaning that his physical appearance has to be unmatched and I long to just gaze upon him every chance I get.

- Faithful- meaning that he only has eyes for me. He would never disrespect me by entertaining another person.

- Financially Secure- I would prefer wealth over riches because there is a huge difference. I would love to see him with that generational wealth instead of the generational curse that most men seem to bring to the table.

- Funny- meaning that he knows what makes me laugh. Laughter is a huge thing in a relationship. I don't need someone who ONLY thinks THEY are funny, believe it or not many comedians suffer from that disease. They think everything that comes out of their mouth is fall over funny but get real stiff lipped when someone else is making a joke. I need someone who can laugh at others but most importantly at themselves.

- Fuck Master- meaning I need a man that knows how to PUT IT DOWN and knows it! There is nothing worse than being with a man who is looking at you for reassurance or acknowledgement. Fool I didn't bring no "Good Job" stickers with me today to stick on your forehead. Nor am I about to pat you on your back and tell you GOOD JOB especially if you've wasted yet another five minutes of my life. I wish I knew how I felt on the inside because whatever it is I'd like to cut it out and just put it back in for the finale. I have been with more men who can't last past the five minute mark that it's exasperating. I am not the one for second chances either. I've heard that some men "rub one out" before going to meet a woman just to ensure longevity, so if you don't have sense enough to do that before you come...I don't know what to tell you. I need a man that has the ability to bring the FREAK out of me. I want to have to take all of the mirrors down in my house the next day to avoid even looking at myself after what I did the night before. In closing, having a beyond decent size "member" would be nice as well.

Comedian Big Sean Larkins walked back on the stage to ask if everyone was having a good time. As the crowd roared "YES" he commenced to getting the stage prepared for the finale of the show which they called "The Lying Game". Maybe it was the nine shots but I don't know who or how they transformed that stage to look like damn near the actual set of "The Dating Game". Things were starting to get really fuzzy, so fuzzy that I swore I heard him say my name.

"Can we get Erica Brown to the stage please" he announced over the mic. Honestly after so many shots I truly assumed there had to be another Erica Brown in the house.

"Erica, we don't have all day, get your ass up here"

Sean said as my crew assisted me to the single chair

on the left side of the partition. This is not how I was

planning on showing my new outfit. I don't like being

the center of attention and that's even knowing that

even without trying, I am. I also don't like GAMES. I'm

like D.L Hughley, I quit school because of recess. This

wasn't nobody but that damn Melanie who set this

shit up. The sad part is that I have no reason to even

try and weasel out of it being that I'm the only single

person in the entire joint tonight.

I take a deep breath and proceed on the stage to the

single chair. On the other side of the partition there

are three other chairs, I just wonder who's going to be

sitting in them. Sean begins the show after the roar of

the crowd settles.

"Tonight we have a treat for you all because this beautiful young lady is a close and personal friend of mine. Would you mind introducing yourself" Sean says as he prompts me to speak into the mic.

It takes me a minute because like I said I am a little inebriated from all of the shots forced down my throat and I loathe being put on the spot. "Good evening, my name is Erica Brown and I'm 40 years old" I manage to get out.

"Can you tell the crowd a little about yourself and try to make it good because your Mr. Wonderful just might be sitting on the other side of this wall. I'm not trying to tell you to sell yourself but at least make the ad look good if you know what I'm saying" Sean said. "Yes, I think I got it. As I said my name is Erica Brown originally from Detroit, Michigan now residing in Atlanta, Georgia. I have a wonderful family which are here with me tonight. Family is number one in my book, so family over all else is my motto. I am a successful business owner that has never been married, by choice. I am silly, witty and yes these are my real titties (*the crowd loses it as I make them bounce up and down*). Financially I have my own, so I don't need yours, however, please don't think that you can come to the table empty handed because as I say all of the time I have no problem eating alone. I'm a certified Life Coach who is actually still trying to get her life together as we speak. I'm passionate and I enjoy doing new things and I'm currently FREE! Debt free, Child free, STD free and Man free". I guess I can throw in there that I'm a comedian too because the room is crying with laughter. I close my little soliloquy with a quick "thank you" and sit back nervous and anxious, not knowing what's in store. I hate the feeling of not knowing...and NO I am NOT a control freak!

"Well you sound like a lot to deal with Erica, which explains why you might be single but that's just me. Now let's meet the three gentlemen who will be fighting to the death for the chance to take you out on the town, right outside those doors at one of the food trucks of your choice sponsored by "Café Cup of Joe". Let's meet them right now...

Contestant number one hails from Decatur, Georgia and tells us that he is a single father of two who loves long quiet walks in the park. Which correlates to he got some bad ass kids and whenever he can get away, he does. He's an electronic engineer which means he has the skinny on the best porn sites on the web because he visits them daily". Sean walks over to him and whispers into the microphone, "Bruh we need to talk later because I've been running across the most

God awful sites. I mean these bitches look like they

got AARP cards and coin slots in their back. I need

some quality hoes. But we'll talk later". Sean walks

back over near me, "I apologize Erica, this is about you

tonight, not me, let me stay focused". I laugh at this

goofy fool because at the same time he's handing the

guy on the other side of this screen a napkin and pen

so he can write down those websites.

"Contestant number two claims that he is an avid

world traveler with no kids" Sean walks back over to

the guys and places his hand on his shoulder "Now let

me ask you this contestant #2, is not having kids and

just saying you don't have kids the same thing,

because I personally know three of your baby mamas?

I just need to get this straight before we move

forward. You know what don't even answer that as a

matter of fact scratch that from the record. The audience will ignore what I just said" he continues to say as he acts like he's in open court and there is a court recorder sitting out there somewhere. "Contestant number two tells us that he is a business owner who likes to drive" Sean laughs out loud and turns to the guy. Now I get it, you're an Uber driver. I swear this damn company has niggas thinking they own their own business just because they driving folks around. Back in the day guys would claim to be one of three things; they were either a drug dealer, barber or rapper. I've met more niggas in the studio than I care to count. Ain't produced a track since the cassette. If you don't get your, wanna be rapping, Easter rhyme having ass somewhere" he says. I am literally crying real tears over here because I agree 100% with what he's saying. Sean continues "last time you had a demo

I had to stick the eraser end of a pencil in it to rewind it and blow it like a Nintendo cartridge. You know what, we gon call you Mario: We didn't give you a name yet so I'm just gonna call you Steve, Steve No Jobs, that's who you are. Your nickname is carpal tunnel...and you know why too" Sean smirked as he said it.

I can't deal with this damn man, he had to be a funny ass child. From Sean's description I honestly don't think I want to get to know any of these men, but this is the LYING GAME which means you don't know what to believe. "Okay, settle down people, pull yourselves together we're trying to help Erica find true love while y'all in here playing around, this is someone's life" Sean yells like he is chastising the crowd. "Simmer down you damn home wreckers! Let's move on to contestant number three. Contestant number three tell us that he is a nurse" Sean abruptly stops talking

and just stares into the audience before he begins

again "Okay, Erica he might be telling the truth

because who in their right mind would claim to be a

male nurse. Nigga, if you ain't a doctor then you're a

patient, nothing else matters after that. Did you just

tell all these damn people that you were a candy

striper? I really don't think that anything else on this

card is even relevant. You can't tell folks that you're a

male nurse. You would have been better off saying

you were a janitor. Take the wheel Jesus. Anyway

y'all, he said he loves to read, cook and has a mean

shoe collection" Sean throws his cards up in the air

and they cascade all over the floor. One of the

waitresses retrieve the cards and hands them back to

Sean who has since taken a seat in the audience

appearing that he has totally given up. After a few

minutes he reluctantly gets back up and walks over to me as he places his hand on my shoulder. With a serious look on his face he says "I'm sorry Erica, you don't deserve this and I want you to understand that this does NOT have a reflection on our friendship. I know it seems like I hate you right now, but I don't. I love you and again, I'm sorry". From this point I stopped taking this serious and decided to just have fun. Sean finally explains that the game will consist of three questions that have been supplied by your family and friends. See, now this is that bullshit. My family and friends don't know what I need. I'm almost in my feelings before I remind myself that this is just a game. I'm not expecting to meet my husband in here, not with these clowns.

"Question number one" says my sister, the culprit herself stands and speaks into the mic. Melanie starts off "Contestant Number One, what is your idea of a

perfect first date"? "Well, a perfect first date would

consist of trying a new restaurant and maybe dancing

afterwards" he says in a squeaky voice like he hasn't

yet hit puberty. "Thank you; same question

Contestant Number Two" Melanie chimes in. "If we

are talking about anything goes then I would say we

could charter a private jet and have dinner on the

beach in Belize. Afterwards we could take the yacht

out to a secluded island where a small table and two

chairs is sitting along the shoreline. The table would

be filled with a variety of finger desserts that would

tickle the taste buds of anyone and finally sip on the

finest wine while we dance slowly under the

moonlight" said contestant number two. The

audience goes wild as they swallow up this well

scripted fantasy that he's feeding them. Boy BYE!

Sean chimes in as he brings the crowd to order

"Damn, brother you trying to get her and every other

lady up in here. The boys got the gift of gab.

Contestant number Three please answer the question.

". "I honestly believe that you shouldn't go all out on

your first date, just keep it simple and let things

escalate from there. Lead up to the good stuff"

confidently said contestant number three. It appears

that contestant number three just can't do anything

right tonight because Sean lays into him after that.

"See, this the shit I'm talking about. Erica this nigga

talking about taking you to the cafeteria in the damn

hospital. Excuse me ma'am sir your bedside bed pan

manners are just not doing it for me tonight. Please

exit my stage right now". Sean said with such disgust.

The man laughs and leaves the stage. When he comes

into light I see that he is a very tall caramel man with a

beautiful physique. He looks like he works out nine days a week. He winks at me as he kisses my hand before he sits in the audience. I think I might be kinda salty about losing this one. He looks like he would have been a lot of fun in bed...damn it man! The game continues as my mother stands and ask the next question. "Bachelor number two, would you be opposed to the woman paying for the date or the majority of the bills at home" my mother says. Sounding about like how I feel. "I'm a firm believer that you should let a woman do what she desires, although it's not something that I would require, if she feels strongly about it then so be it. I'll look for other ways to return the favor" contestant number two says without missing a beat. I don't know whether to think he's broke or he really believes in equality. Contestant number one interjects "No, absolutely not. If I'm her man then that's what I will be. I don't believe that a woman should be responsible for paying the bills and providing. I'll do all the heavy lifting and she can maintain the home like the bible says". Now as crazy as this sounds I'm not really feeling his answer because some women like to work, they love their careers. I most certainly don't want to be a sit at home mom, cooking and cleaning like some damn beckon call girl. I know what the bible says but hell times have changed. I think I'm still looking too deep into this since it's only a game.

Sean stands up and moves back to the front of the stage before he speaks "Okay everyone the last question of the night comes from Charmone". "Alright, this question is actually from all of us and each of you will have to write your answers down on the board provided" Charmone said as she pointed to a small white dry erase board and marker under our

chairs. "Erica, you have to write your answer down as

well. You will be writing down what you HOPE they

say" she continued. "You will all hold your answers up

at the same time when prompted to do so,

understand"? Everyone nods as she commences to

reading the final question. Okay, on a scale from one

to ten please rate yourself sexually and please keep in

mind that your number should actually match the

length of your penis". The crowd is literally in tears

right about now. I swear I don't know how I stayed

friends with these hoes all this time. I am so

embarrassed right now that it's not even funny. I'm

glad that red and orange go well together because I

know that my entire face is on fire! "Please remember

to be HONEST. There is no right or wrong answer,

unless your answer is anywhere below six. If that's the

case please take your vagina and exit stage left...we'll wait" Sean said. From the laughter in the audience, apparently one of the guys stood up to act like he was walking off the stage. I really wish I could see these dudes. "Gentlemen and Ladies please hold up your answers" Charmone said with a giggle. I don't know what those two over there wrote down but I wrote down the number eleven. The crowd stood to their feet with excitement as Sean fell to the floor. I wish I could see what was on their boards. Sean composes himself and finally says to the audience "In the center of the table you will see three colored paddles associated with the colored background behind each contestant. Fortunately you only have to choose from two contestants because our third contestant had to go and change his maxi pad. So please, hold up your paddles now". Sean scans the room doing an unofficial count but from the looks of it whoever is BLUE has pretty much swept the room. "Alright, alright, let me introduce you to the man you will NOT be sharing a basket of fries and a large coke with...with two straws. His real name is Adonis. Adonis please walk around and meet who could have been your kids' step-mom" Sean says as the audience claps. A short and stout man walks around the partition holding up a sign with the number SEVEN written on it. We hug and he continues on to a seat in the audience. "Now let's meet the guy that the audience picked for you. His name is Eddie. Eddie please come on over and meet Ms. Erica Brown. To my shock, surprise and delight Edward walks around the partition dressed in a black suit and black collared shirt with no tie. He looks like he just jumped off the cover of GQ! We both smile at each other and I drown in his massive arms as the crowd cheers and we exit through the front door.

We both kinda just stand there and grin mischievously. But before a single word can be uttered we are approached by a nerdy looking white guy in a shirt and tie who taps Edward on his shoulder. He apologizes for interrupting and continues "Edward, I know this is horrible timing but if I could steal you away for about thirty minutes to get some of these orders taken care of I would appreciate it. I wouldn't bother you but you see the crowd, it's crazy in there and we are short staffed" he uttered as he quickly walks away.

"Wow" was the only thing that Edward could muster. He looked defeated again. "Apparently I'm needed in there. If you could give me thirty minutes I'll be right back. Go ahead and order whatever you like, it's on the house" he said as he walked away. Just like a

broke man to ball out on another person's tab. I

ordered something to go because I'm tired and I'm

not sticking around for thirty minutes just to continue

to hear more of this wild fantasy first date he was

talking about it. I order a Philly Cheesesteak and fries,

tell my friends and family bye and walk home. It's only

a few blocks anyway. The weather is nice and I could

use the alone time to clear my head.

As tough as relationships are wouldn't you like a little reassurance in making that **GREAT** relationship **PERFECT**?

Ever considered using an external "helping hand"?

"You've Got Love" is a revolutionary product and system that can help with just about any relationship.

Learn more by visiting our website

www.*ThePlayGirl*.org

Chapter Seven

Compromising Does NOT Mean Settling

I knew that it was a bad idea to drink last night and drink so much at that. Trust me, even with the amount of liquor in my house it is actually only for show. I haven't met a bottle of wine that I could finish. I wake up well past my scheduled time and the only reason that I'm not freaking out right now is because it's a Monday and I don't have any appointments scheduled. I do have our Monday morning staff meeting but I gave Ashlyn a heads up that I might not be in today. I think Jasmine, Brittany **@calypsosway** and She'mia **@_mamamia2u** can hold it down until my body releases me from the merry-go-round that I'm trapped on. It's like when I have my horrible migraines (*thanks to my father*), once I throw up I know I'll feel much better. I drag myself out of bed and on all fours crawl over to the bathroom to pray to the porcelain God. Every muscle in my body feels like it went three rounds with Mayweather or Tyson. I hate myself this morning because I never drink and now we know why.

Today I am really considering putting on some sweats and gym shoes and concurring the world from the depths of hell where I'm at, but that's not how I got to where I am right now. I have to suck it up and put on my big girl panties. I walk into my closet after I get out of the shower. I opted for a quick and cold shower and not a bath to decrease the chances of drowning. Something that most people don't know about me is that you can tell exactly how I feel by how I dress. You know how most people get dressed all the way up when they are feeling their best, well, I'm just the opposite? When I feel my worst that's normally when I do my best and go all out. Some days when I wake up and look in the mirror it feels like something is missing, maybe a nose or my eyes or maybe even my mouth...but something is amiss. Which means that I have to really over compensate to make things balance out and be able to feel confident when I look in the mirror. That means hair, make-up and outfit have to be STUNNING! On those days I will have on a FULL face of make-up. On the days when I'm happy with the refection I will still dress nice but my make-up will be minimal, because I feel like there is no need to try too hard. Now, on the days where I wake up and my skin is flawless, I'm glowing, cheeks are rosy (*both of them*) there's a pep in my step, the tits are headed North as appose to South, it's a good hair day and my iron is relatively high then you will see me at my most comfortable. I'll probably have on some jeans with a blazer, an offensive tee and some heels. Hair back in a ponytail, Vaseline on my lips and a little eyeliner...but that's all. From the outside looking in others may think it's a dress down day when in reality it's a "don't have to try because I'm 100% happy with the original me" day. It might not make sense right now but it will. Just think about it, when you're feeling flawless, what's the point of adding anything else? Then there are days like today when the reflection in the mirror has its back to you because that's how bad you look and feel. On those days for the safety of others it's probably best to climb back in bed and start over tomorrow. If it weren't for the fact that I have a super busy week and I'm a workaholic I would do just that.

Invention of a Man

It's a beautiful day to walk to the office so I don't even consider calling my driver. I am wrestling with my inner me trying to decide if I want to stop and get something to eat and my morning coffee but then I think about running into Edward again and that settles that debate. Besides, I can always send Ashlyn on a coffee run if I can't hold off until lunch. I probably couldn't hold anything down anyway. I wait at this traffic light praying that it hurries up. I've never wanted to see this white man so bad in my life! I would take my chances Jay walking but you can't trust Atlanta drivers on a good day. When a state only requires a driver to take a driving test in an empty parking lot and NOT on an actual street, you just know that once that real life video game starts it's GAME OVER...I'll wait.

The office is relatively quiet when I walk in, maybe they had the meeting without me, which is fine because I can just go over the minutes. I stop at the receptionist desk to speak with Ashlyn and she is looking beautiful as usual. She has on a blue dress with a décor of different buttons. She seems distant today, not that she has an attitude or being short or cold, but I can just tell. I know she's a big girl but I would be lying if I said it didn't concern me a little.

"Ashlyn, when you get a moment come into my office" I said before I started to walk away. "As a matter of fact can you do a coffee run before you do that please" she interrupts me before I could even tell her what I want. "Actually, about ten minutes ago a courier dropped off coffee and pastries for the entire staff. Along with that Edible Arrangement sitting on your desk" she said as she smiled and held up her coffee and half eaten pastry. Ashlyn got up from behind her desk taking my purse and bag out of my hand and started walking with me toward my office. She grabbed the door and held it open as I walked thru. Maybe she really needed to talk this morning.

"First and Foremost let me say that you look beautiful today" I say from under an intoxicated smile. "Thank you ma'am, you know I try" she says and then gets quiet. "You know I know when something is wrong with you so spill the beans little girl. You get all of this advice for free, so use me up. What's going on" I ask.

"I swear it feels crazy to even say that I have relationship problems working in this environment. But I do and I am so conflicted right now that it's making me sick. I didn't tell you that I met someone new, right" she said. I'm sure she's not looking for an actual response because she knows good and damn well she didn't tell me about meeting anyone new.

Last I heard she was dating some guy that played for

the Green Bay Packers, I think that's the right team.

I'm not into sports unless you call looking at their

butts a sport, then I'm a fan. I can't think of the name

right now but I do know that he played ball and if I

remember correctly this wasn't the only athlete she

was talking to. I told her then to be careful about

playing the field; that it might be safer to come off the

"field" and head over to the "court" at least, unless of

course she took my advice about just being upfront

and honest with everyone. It's much easier to be

honest than to be a player. I simply shook my head no

and allowed her to keep talking. I know when to be

quiet which makes me a great listener. "Well,

remember I was talking to old boy from the Cowboys,

well, that didn't work out. It actually didn't work out

with any of them, so I cut everyone off, at least

sexually I did. I still need to keep it friendly just in case

we need tickets for something. But I took your advice

and decided to just work on me. You told me that if

every relationship fails it might not be them and that I

should try looking in the mirror, so I did. When I

cleared the bench and was forced to only deal with

me I saw that I had a lot to work on and that's what I

did and became the best ME that I could be. For the

longest time I was only motivated by money, cars and

who could offer me that kind of life. With no one but

YOU to have to answer to you see things a bit clearer.

I learned that I'm no longer the girl that needed to

build a man and that maybe if I couldn't find

everything in one person or could find most of what I

needed, then I could find happiness. I did what you

said and started looking for the things that I would

NOT accept instead of the things that made me smile in the moment like looks, money and sex. They all seem so superficial when you start to only deal with the facts. It turned out that the guys who could offer me the world actually had more things that I would NOT deal with than things I would, shit's crazy. It made me start to broaden the playing field and by doing that it opened the door to meet guys that I would have never given the time of day" she got quiet and looked off into the distance. I decided to chime in to give her a minute to get her thoughts together before she spoke again. "So it appears that you met someone who at one point in time you would have considered beneath you and you are at a crossroad because you don't know if you should open up completely and a part of you wants to retreat back to what's familiar. Am I warm"? "Yes, Lord yes" she mumbled. "I take it he has a regular every day job and simple life and that scares you" I continued. "Regular job is putting it lightly honestly. I'm not tripping hell look at me, it's not like I'm a damn doctor or lawyer. I don't have it going on like you. I'm just regular old Ashlyn" she said. "And nothing's wrong with that" I interjected. "I know, and trust me it's not just that, he has dreams, but he's not just a dreamer. I remember you told me to be careful with guys who have "potential" because sometimes that's all they have at the end of the day. But he's different. We have been talking for about seven months and he is so supportive. He stays on me when it comes to me reaching the goals that I've told him about. He calls me every afternoon to see how my day is going and to see what I've done to get closer to my dreams. He's handsome and sexy, not rich but will give me his last and has shown me that it doesn't take a million dollars to have a great time. He even has me going to church. Me, church, can you believe it" she laughed. Ashlyn probably goes to church less than I do and that speaks volumes.

"So, no more roster, no starting five. Just me and him" she said with a look of bewilderment on her face like she couldn't even believe she was saying it herself.

"Then what's the problem" I asked? "I guess what worries me is if this is just a phase I'm going thru and he's just a trial. I don't want him caught up in my building process. Because trust me when I tell you that there are times that I'm a bit touched if I don't get a certain item or we can't afford to go to a certain event because he doesn't have the money. I don't want to get all the way into this and start having regrets" she said. "So, you're telling me that you don't know how to deal with obstacles as they come? You're saying that you're afraid to fail and have to start again with a new plan or approach to get the results that you desire? Are you saying that you can't treat? Sometimes you have to do something different to get different results. There's no master plan in relationships, you have to do what works best for you. Money, looks and material things aren't everything, they matter, but they're not the end all to be all. It's as simple as that. The only people that you are trying to make happy is you and your partner, no one else is in bed with you. There's no such thing as losing as long as there was a lesson learned" and I ended the conversation with that. I'm guessing that Ashlyn got what she needed from that conversation because she stood up and headed for the door. Just before leaving she turned and said "So happiness trumps everything". It was more of a question than anything. "As long as you're not hurting YOU or anyone else and you're not LOSING more than you gain then the house always wins" I said without even looking up from my desk. With that said she returned to the reception area. I finally looked at the card on the "Edible Arrangement" to see who sent it. This is actually perfect because now I have something to eat for breakfast including the pastries and stuff. The card read...

"You robbed me of my date and I think you owe me now. Have dinner with me again. I'd like to take you somewhere special"

ES

I guess it doesn't take much to make me smile these days because I'm grinning from ear to ear. I grab my phone and text Edward a simple "Yes" and leave it at that. The ball is in his court. I think back to what Ashlyn and I talked about and think that it's time that I start talking the talk and walking the walk, something that I don't normally do. When I think about it, each time that we've met, although it hasn't been a five star restaurant or dining experience Edward was the one who picked up the bill. I am a person who loves the finer things in life and I have no problem with paying for it. I grab my phone again and text Edward back. "Since I'm the one who stood you up allow me to treat you. I insist and remember you said that if a woman insist you would oblige" I press send and wait patiently for his response as I continue on with the rest of my day. I don't even notice that I missed his reply until I look back up at the clock to see that it's almost the end of the day. I didn't want to be a bother because I didn't know if he was at work and couldn't have his phone on him. Juggling hot coffee and texting is possible but why chance getting burned or in trouble. I actually have twenty-two missed calls, text and emails. I look at my phone and see that I hadn't turned my ringer back on from last night. Anyway, Edward reluctantly agreed to my request, now I have to move quickly. He said that he would be free tomorrow night by six o'clock. I wanted to be innovative because I honestly loved the dates that he came up with using what little resources he had. You have to admire a man who can do that. I saw a meme on Instagram the other day of a man on the train with a "Hot-n-Ready" pizza from Little Caesar and a store bought bouquet of flowers. Like clockwork the majority of the comments were negative, taunting him for the simplistic gesture that he was making.

Saying how they wish a nigga would show up at their door with a pizza and Kroger flowers. It honestly disgusted me and what's crazy is that most of the females commenting probably don't even have anyone in their lives that would buy their asses a slice of cheese pizza and a single stem plastic carnation. The guys commenting wouldn't know how to approach a real lady from behind the security of social media if given the opportunity anyway. Using your resources and creating the best with what you have doesn't make you a loser. Not making the effort and dogging someone else who is taking the initiative; that's what makes you a sad case or bum...loser! The only problem that I saw with the picture was that he had the flowers laying on top of the box which would more than likely make them wilt quicker from the heat from the "Hot-n-Ready" pizza. Outside of that, great job Romeo, I would be ever so giddy if you were my suitor. Now, let me see what I can come up with on such short notice.

I suddenly remembered about a new restaurant that just opened called "Pot Luck" in Atlanta. The owner is a gentlemen named Charles or "Chef Tru" **@chef_tru** and his concept is unforgettable. I've only been a few times with my girls but it's exactly what it sounds like. Each guest brings some sort of food item and pay ten dollars to get in. You are seated with others to combine a five star meal and dine together. You determine what meat you'd like and trust the talented chef to do the rest. I've never had a bad meal I can tell you that. It's virtually impossible to get a reservation but that's if you don't know the owner. It doesn't hurt that I assisted him in finding the woman that he's married to right now. After you are seated with your group, normally people you don't know unless you

make your reservations for a specific party; you are

required to pay for your drinks and to tip your chef

and waitress. They also have a very sophisticated

dessert menu. It's probably one of the most unique

dining experiences that I've ever had. I give Charles a

call directly to set up dinner reservations for

tomorrow at nine o'clock. He pens me in for two

people and I thank him before I hang up. Edward

hasn't told me where he lives yet. I'm guessing after

seeing my place he might not be too eager to give me

a tour of his living space, I guess we'll cross that bridge

when we get to it. I send Edward another text

requesting him to be at my house no later than eight. I

ask Ashlyn to set up transportation for tomorrow. If I

had been thinking I would have asked her to join us

along with her new boo and just made reservations

Nedra Simone

for four since she said they haven't really been able to

go out and have a night out on the town. Although it's

not expensive to begin with it would have been my

treat and a new experience. I make a note to treat the

staff and few others next month. That way I'm

supporting a friend and treating those who are my

backbone to a night out on the town. Okay,

reservations have been made and the transportation

is secured. I'm in the treating mood so I take it a step

further and call Charles back to see what he thought

about having a live set tomorrow, my treat. I know

that funds can be tight when you are first starting out

in a business venture. From his excitement I take it as

a yes. I hang up and put a request out to one of my

favorite indie artist. I could ask someone who has

already made it but why...bless someone else

whenever you can. I call a good friend, Ray Rush

@iamrayrush and see if he's available tomorrow night and if he could get a band together. Ray is the kind of friend that would do it for me for free, but again I ask...why. Ray tells me that he's actually supposed to be rehearsing with a guy named "Raybone" **@raysoloiam** tonight and tomorrow, so it works out perfectly. The crazy thing is I think I know him from back in the day and if it's the same guy he is a phenomenal singer. Those two together is a recipe for wet panties and goosebumps. I tell him the more the merrier and ask if I could book a female singer with them. A good friend of mine, Dawn, **@thedawnmichele** is always down for a jam session. He agrees and I send her a text to see if she's free tomorrow night and if she'd be interested. Just as I thought she says yes. Out of all my homies Dawn is the most reliable person I know with the exception of my besties Tabitha **@tabithastallings** and Sheric. I

only have a handful of true friends and these ladies

don't even have the seniority that my other girls have

but those three have earned the title of RIDE or DIE! I

give Dawn Ray's contact and suggest that she reaches

out to him because they are actually rehearsing

tonight and if she's not busy she could join them, but

it turns out that they already know each other; I

should have known.

Edward replies back with a simple "Okay, see you

then". Good, my work here is done.

Like clockwork Edward shows up at eight on the dot

looking and smelling good. He is casually dressed in

dark jeans, a button up stripped button up shirt and

blazer. I give him a quick hug and a peck on the cheek.

I'm ready with the exception of my shoes and purse. I

never wear shoes in the house, I hate that. It always

feels like you're ready to go, relax, take your shoes

off; stay awhile. I grab my things and join Edward

again who is still standing by the elevator gate. When

we get in the elevator her leans in to tell me how

gorgeous I look tonight. He also slides in that if I taste

as good as I smell then he hopes that I'm on the menu

tonight. As quickly as he blurts it out he apologizes for

being so crass. However, I like my men straight

forward with a hint of bad boy. You can be a

gentlemen without being a scary punk. I am

completely turned off by guys who don't take charge

and ask for what they want. Don't send me a text

after I leave saying what you "would" have done.

Sorry but you missed your opportunity and after so

many false starts it will only secure you a spot in the

"Friend Zone" please have several seats Mr. TOO Nice

Guy! "No need to apologize, you never know if you

don't ask and it helps to know where your appetite is and I love a man with a healthy appetite" I say seductively as we approach the car. Standing on the sidewalk is an impeccably dressed Justin. I catch the whiff of Ivory soap and cocoa butter, no cologne tonight, which means that he doesn't have a date. Men are such simple creatures. "Good evening Justin, how was your day" I ask? "It was wonderful thank you for asking. I hope you had a beautiful day as well" he said in return. "I did, and I pray that it continues on through the night" I say. "Well I'm sure it will, you're definitely in good hands with Mr. Sparks" he shakes Edwards hand and we both get in the car. They must have met before he came into the building. They seem so familiar with each other but that's the feeling I get every time I've been out with Edward, like the man has no enemies and makes friends with everyone he meets. That's a good sign if you ask me. Yet another

great quality to look for in someone.

It's about a thirty minute drive to "Pot Luck" and as

usual it is packed. When we pull up Justin exits the car

and walks around to open our door. It's a very nice

night with the exception of a slight breeze. I would say

that I am sexy-casual tonight; dressed in a two-piece

set from a boutique my cousin Tameka runs on

Instagram, **@lavispieces70**. I actually saw Marjorie

Harvey wear it and knew from that moment that I had

to have it. It's a rayon and spandex blend, a shiny

silver leggings with a floor length matching jacket.

Now, when Mrs. Harvey wore it she played it safe with

a very conservative top underneath, however; I'm not

her and I'm wearing just the contents of the package.

Luckily for me I still have the kind of breast that stand

at attention instead of at ease. You see, I know that

gravity has no friends and I plan to take advantage of that for as long as I possibly can because once I can tuck them into my pants I won't be able to pull this look off. From the way that Edward hasn't been able to take his eyes off of me I feel safe assuming that I pulled this look off. He might as well thank my fashion muse for this one and several others, so thank you in advance Mrs. Harvey, because of you I might be getting me some tonight.

When we enter the place there is a buzz in the air, the band in jamming and the smell is to die for. When we check in we are promptly escorted to our table where the waitress takes our food items and carries them to the kitchen. Here the chef actually cooks in front of you like at a Hibachi restaurant. They do most of the prep work in the kitchen and the remainder of the cooking at your table.

Edward pulls my chair out and waits until I'm seated before taking a seat himself. We introduce ourselves to the rest of our dinner guest and commence to enjoying the band and singers while dinner is prepared. As usual I get a special shout out from the band during their set. When I tell you that they are jamming tonight! It's crazy how quickly they put together a show in such short notice. That just shows you that they are true professionals. It sounds like they've been singing together forever. I swear I love talented people and the world is filled with them just waiting for their chance. "Are you enjoying yourself Edward" I ask, knowing full well that he is because he's been singing along since we walked in and he doesn't have a bad voice either. "I could sit in a windowless room with you folding laundry and I could manage to have a good time. It's not always about the location; more about the company if you ask me" he said as he continued to watch the band. Although he wasn't looking at me I could tell that he could still see me...emotionally. Our meal consisted of both chicken and steak, stuffed baked potatoes with spicy Italian sausages and peppers sitting on a bed of angel hair sweet potato pasta. The appetizers are stuffed mushrooms along with raw vegetable tray. I cannot wait to dig in. It's amazing how these chefs come up with these spontaneous meals on the spot not knowing what they have to work with. What if someone brought a can of "Spam" and someone else brought a pack of hotdogs. That would be damn interesting and I'd be excited to see what they might come up with. You're definitely taking a chance when you eat here but the chefs he has employed here have to be part-time magicians as well and they also have to love a challenge. After dinner our waitress brings out assorted finger desserts which in no way disappoints. When you leave here you are full, I'll tell you that damn much. I'm so comfortable with this man that I actually fall asleep on the ride home in his arms. I don't wake up until we pull up in front of my building. The cool air from outside wakes me when Justin opens the door. "Mr. Sparks will you be needing a ride home sir" Justin asks without being prompted. When I see Edward hesitate I reply for him "No, that will actually be all for the evening Justin. Have a wonderful remainder of the night". "Not a problem ma'am and if anything changes don't hesitate to contact me. Have a good evening and thank you very much Mr. Sparks" he said before he walked around to get back in the car and drive off into the night. He still has enough time to get into something if he wants.

See, I'm looking out for everyone tonight.

Edward and I step into the elevator and ride up to the second floor quietly. I'm hoping that I've placed enough subliminal hints that he can relax and let himself go, because the answer tonight to all of his questions is yes. We walk into the living room and before I can take another step I see Edward lean up against the wall and just stare at me. I can feel his eyes burning a hole in my skin as I turn to face him. With no words said he removes his jacket and shirt and just before I can untie the belt to my coat he stops me as he grabs my hand softly and places it back by my side. I follow his silent orders and continue to enjoy his glare as he undresses me with his eyes. What he revealed under that shirt is nothing short of amazing. Imagine hills and mountains of smooth chocolate that seem to go on for days. The hue is reminiscent of the sun shining just enough for the chocolate to begin to melt causing it to glisten and sparkle at the surface; except this light is actually that of the moon sitting directly outside the window as if it was designed specifically for us and this exact moment. He unfastens the button to his pants and slowly lets the zipper cascade down in an almost hypnotic motion. Right about now all I can think of is Renee Zellweger in the movie "Jerry Maguire", you had me at hello. As he walks over to me it feels like my insides are actually reeling him in. The physical connection is undeniable. As he stands in front of me his eyes looking at the top of my head while mine focus on his beautiful chest. He takes his hand and lifts my chin up to face him as he kisses me ever so slowly and passionately. The warmth of his mouth and sensual movement of his tongue traps me in a mental trance caught somewhere between "Fifty Shades and Zane". Just when I think he's about to swoop me up off my feet, he doesn't; instead he takes hold of the belt holding my coat together and leads me to my bedroom and sits upon my bed as I stand in front of him. "I want to remember every second of this so please don't rush" he said. It didn't take a rocket scientist to know that he wanted me to undress for him and to take my time while doing it. Before I start to undress I walk over to the radio and turn on my Pandora, setting it to smooth R&B. I dance erotically to Bell Biv Devoe's "I do need you" as I slowly untie the knot holding my coat together allowing my body to control the pace of his heartrate. I use the length of the coat to hide parts of my body that I'm not ready to show during this peep show. When I determine that's enough I let it fall to the floor around my feet. I walk

over to where he is sitting on the bed and playfully

use my hair to caress his body. Not about to be the

only one standing here exposed I squat down and slip

his shoes and socks off and next his pants. I am

ecstatic to see that he's not wearing tighty whiteys

because that would have killed the entire mood. I can

deal with the boxer briefs that he has on. I actually

really like them because it shows the erect goodness

of what's to come. Still no words are said with our

mouths but I'm telling a hell of a story with my body.

He breaks code and attempts to reach out for me but I

put a stop to that quickly. You requested this tease

and a tease is what you shall get, or at least as long as

I can take it. After a few minutes I move away and

slowly remove my leggings that have been acting like

a second skin for me. Like I said earlier this outfit is to

die for. Like any real man should he soon took control of the situation and pulled me into him and with such strength that it actually took me by surprise. In one fell swoop I was in the air my landing place being on his lap perched upon his mighty tool that I was beyond eager to place inside my toolbox. Damn a sixty day rule like Steve Harvey suggested (*although it is awesome advice*) I know what I want and right now it is Edward Sparks. Before I know it I am lying on my back as he ventures down to remove my lace panties using only his teeth. In the heat of the moment I completely forgot to even ask about contraceptives, but like he was reading my mind he stops for just enough time required to retrieve one from the pocket in his pants. All the while I'm repeating in my mind "Please let it be GOLD, Please let it be GOLD" I guess someone knew they were getting lucky tonight. Cocky or confident I'm glad that he took the initiative and that I didn't have to ask. Standing over me he removes his briefs to reveal something that honestly should have come with a warning. I don't know if I need to stretch me LEGS or my MOUTH. This is one of those situations where you almost want to back out of what's about to go down. I'm just glad that I hadn't been talking shit up until this point. However, it's still early and I've been with guys who could use their dicks to pole vault with but ended up performing like they were playing putt-putt golf. With the lack luster performance they should have been given the proper equipment and called it what it was, miniature golf. Other times I've been with guys who acted like they were oblivious to what they possessed and treated you like a man with a six inch cock. I mean ramming me to the point that I thought I'd require reconstructive surgery or that I was going to need to have a custom curtain made because this bastard done blew a hole through my back and now I have a window. Not Edward though, when he entered me he did it with such ease filling up every square inch of real estate inside of me. I mean this man moved in a way that should have been illegal in 59 states (*realize that I added some more because that was just how great it was*). With every thrust I would have taken residency inside of a cramped bottle and became his genie if he would have asked. At this point I know that we are compatible sexually, I love his company and conversation and oddly enough his career level is not even phasing me; but then again that's what good dick does, it clouds your vision; so, I'm honestly happy that I discovered all of this pre-dick. Have you ever had dick that was so good the next thing you know

Invention of a Man

you're waking up the next day, well that's what
happened? Last night's reality seamed effortlessly into
a fantasy. When I opened my eyes I was alone with a
note on the pillow next to me thanking me for a
wonderful evening. I feel like I'm floating right now.
Not only from euphoria but from confusion. Please
don't tell me this was a one-time hit it and quit it kind
of thing. All I could think about is, this must be how
countless guys have felt when I did the same thing to
them.

Just when I thought that I might have found most of
what I desire in one man and could stop the dreaded
cycle of Build-a-Man, I'm left confused and alone; I'm
not sure of what to do now.

Nedra Simone

Write a letter to yourself

Make a promise to yourself...and keep it!

Chapter Eight

W.T.F

Although I'm still skeptical about the other night, life continues to go on. I haven't really spoken to Edward this week, mainly because it has been a very hectic week for me. I don't even know what I was expecting from the other night, I guess you could blame it on HOPE. I was hoping that he might be different from the rest. A think a big part of me is discouraged most because I was prepared to bend my own rules and even lower my expectations when it came to him. But hey, it is what it is, right. I am a firm believer that you can get over ANYONE in seven days. Shit, if God could create this beautiful world in seven days (*actually six*) then a person can get over another person with no problem. I forgot that I told my sister and them that I would throw a game party tonight. It's not like I was planning on doing anything with my Saturday but my anti-social side is present and I would much rather sit at home and just "wished" I had gone out. I probably need to work on that in this upcoming year. I'll add it to the list of New Year's Resolutions that I don't plan to fulfill anyway. I've become so last minute lately and honestly it's sickening. I reach out to my cook to see if she's busy tonight for a small get together and luckily she's free. That saves me from having to search for a last minute catering service and my personal chef is the bomb. I am incapable of doing anything "small" and whenever I do have an event, I try to elevate it and make it a place where everyone can present themselves as the creative and business-minded people they are. The days of having people around me who don't have shit or even worse, don't want shit, is over. If you can't support me the same way I do you then what good are you to yourself much less me. Please stand up and give your seat to someone looking to build an empire and then take your ass way over there and have SEVERAL seats in the "I'm just going to sit here and admire all the hard work that other people have done" section. I like to see all of my folks succeed. My girl Charmone is a go-getter, she started her own company and I will support her every chance I can. She creates the most sinful sweets that you've ever had **@sweetsbycharmone**. I just hope that she remembers about bringing them tonight. I will shoot her a text anyway. When I log onto Facebook I see that Melanie has been up since six a.m. inviting people for tonight. From the looks of it I need to tell Chef Michelle to triple those numbers because this crazy broad has made it an open invitation. Just for shits and giggles I extend the invite to Edward via text. This is a dress down event so I'm not worried about my hair too much. I'm about to wash this shit and be done with it. I will probably throw on some silk joggers and a half top. After I send the menu to Chell & Chan (my chefs) I call my favorite karaoke DJ "Stacia and KD" **@staciasuperstar** to see if she can make a miracle happen for me tonight, especially since it's my fault that everything is last minute. I tell her that I'll double her normal rate and although she rejects the offer she won't be able to reject the payment when it hits her PayPal. When you do something good NEVER do it for free UNLESS you're doing it for GOOD...there's the difference. Whenever I have an event I always hire someone to take pictures. It allows people to enjoy themselves while not having to worry about documenting their every moment. My friend

Donnell **@whitemothsociety** is one of the most

talented people I've ever met. I book him every time.

When I get out the shower I hear more than one voice

in the other room, so let me put some clothes on

before I walk out here. I'm confused because no one

else is supposed to be here for at least seven hours. I

walk out to see Michelle & Marchan hard at work in

the kitchen along with my mom and sister. I don't

know why they can't just let these women do their

damn job like they're volunteering or something.

"Good morning all, Michelle, do we have a wait staff

for tonight or do I need to make arrangements" I ask.

"Actually all of that has been taken care of already.

The food is being prepped and I went ahead and set

up a service for an open bar as well" she said. "Girl,

this ain't about to be no damn family reunion or

nothing, this is just for some of our close friends and family" Melanie interrupted like I hadn't seen that seventy-six people had already confirmed via Facebook and Instagram. "Well it was until you turned Facebook into Evite" I snapped back. "I should probably shut that down then" she retorted embarrassingly and retreated to her phone. My mother was laughing as she chopped whatever was sitting in front of her. I walked over and hugged her, something that she hates with a passion. The woman has never done passion or affection of any kind. I don't know how she has intercourse. She probably does it like the folks in the movie "Cocoon". If you've never seen it, I highly recommend it, it's an oldie but a goody. I think my mom's from Venus, I gotta watch her from now on. The intercom buzzes and I walk over to ask who it is. "Yes ma'am, this is your grocery delivery from Sam's Club" he screams into the intercom. I press the button allowing him to come up on the elevator. When the elevator reaches the floor I also see my crew from the café. "What is everyone doing here so early, you all didn't have to help with anything; we could have done it" I said. "So bitch are you saying that you would like us to leave or are you going to grab one of these damn bags" Tabitha says. We all help with the bags and boxes, and an event that would have been stressful because of my lack of enthusiasm during preparation turns out to be a breeze with everyone pitching in. See, that's what I'm talking about, teamwork...and not having to ask for it! I love these hoes! Almost three decades of friendship in one room and we are still going strong. Everyone finds something to do from cooking to decorating to being the unofficial DJ, which is a hard job because it's on you to keep the tempo moving. Luckily for us my place stays clean not to mention the housekeeper was just here two days ago.

As teenagers we used to call our little clique 'B.A.B", to parents and school officials we were known as "Black and Beautiful"; but out and about and around the way we were known as "Bad Ass Bitches". We were something else and with the exception of four or five, the original crew is still together. Some of the ladies fell out, some fell off and some are doing hard time. I guess those truly were bad ass bitches. Now that we are "of age", not that we're old but the knees aren't quite what they used to be. Some of us can still drop it like it's hot while others might need Icy Hot after several failed attempts. We now call ourselves "Social Butterflies" and our get-togethers are a bit more toned down and community responsible...but there will always be "yesterday". Time flies as we party and prepare so quickly that when we look up we only have three hours until party time. Everyone stays relatively close so it's no big deal to run home and get changed and come back.

I'm left with an empty house with the exception of Michelle who is actually out on the balcony having a smoke. Looking at the clock I realize that I still haven't heard back from Edward and although I'm kind of bothered you will never know it unless I tell you. I'm use to this behavior so if nothing less I know how to deal with it. I haven't gotten dirty or anything but I decide to change clothes anyway. I opt for a nice pair of skinny jeans and a funny tee that reads "After Cumming You Should Be Going". I'm a beast in this t-shirt game; and as much as I love shoes when home I am always barefoot whenever I can be.

About forty-five minutes prior to the start of the event the wait staff and DJ arrive **@staciasuperstar**. I love people who are prompt and about their business. Although I know that he will decline my assistance I always ask KD if he needs any help bringing all of the equipment and lights in. Stacia and I take a few minutes to catch up and I do a last once over to make sure that everything is in order. Like clockwork the crew shows back up and the guest start to arrive. I have the game playing on the over-head projector. I could care less for sports but that doesn't mean that I will deny it for others who do. Although I'm not making it obvious I am watching the door to see if Edward does in fact show up. Melanie walks over to me and nudges my arm. "Great turn out so far" she says. I agree but I guess my reply didn't come out how she believed that it should. "Alright, what's wrong" she said as she looked deep into my eyes as if she was looking for something. I guess I can't really hide too much from her. She probably knows me better than anyone. But just because she knows that something is off she doesn't need to know details. "Nothing's wrong, I'm just trying to make sure that things are in order. To be honest I just started working on this this morning, I had forgotten all about it" I said still looking around the room. "Okay, you don't have to tell me, but I will figure it out. You don't have to be ON all of the time. You help everyone around you and steal little pieces of their happiness until you feel content but I've never seen you submerge yourself in your own happiness. Yeah, it's great to fix others and create their happily ever after but there comes a time when you have to focus on you. It's time to stop wearing other people's smiles and get one of your own" she kisses me on the cheek and walks away. No matter how old I am she will always be my big sister and regardless of if she does the complete opposite of what I tell her to do when it comes to relationships she has been known to drop these little jewels of knowledge of her own. For as long as I remember she's been the other woman and quite content at it to be honest. Although she says how much she wants a man of her own and would like a meaningful relationship, sometimes sharing (*or settling*) is easier. When a person puts their all into a relationship and always seem to keep finding the same guy over and over again you can get discouraged and start to believe that this is honestly what the world has to offer...so why try. So it starts there, ignoring your moral compass and accepting fractions of a person instead of demanding the whole person. Next you begin to make excuses for that person and start

convincing yourself that this is what you want. Finally

you start to live contently in this reality that you have

created not realizing that what you have actually

become is scared. Scared to put forth the effort,

scared to waste your time, scared of rejection, scared

of commitment, scared of the responsibility of a

relationship because trust me, one of the best feelings

in the world is the sigh of relief when you're able to

send someone back to their significant other *(by*

choice) after convincing yourself that they are

someone else's problem especially after you have

gotten from them what you needed to fill the empty

hole in you both literally and figuratively. That actually

requires a really strong person to even do this so just

imagine what you could get out of a friendship and/or

relationship if you harnessed that energy into the

thing that you truly want and that's to be loved by one person unconditionally…but people will change only when they are ready and that comes with loving yourself first. Because let's face it, how can you really love someone else if you don't even love yourself?

While several of the guys (*and gals*) are watching the game another group is forming to play a new card game that we found a few months ago called "W.T.F" (*no it's now what you first initially think*) it's actually "Words That Fit". I have played hundreds of games in my lifetime but this game trumps them all. Every time we play the game someone will notice another game that they've played that reminds them of it. I swear it is so many games wrapped up in one and it's actually for ALL ages. Their tagline is "From the Classroom to the Bedroom" and they are so right. The game mirrors the personalities that are playing it so it can be sweet, innocent and educational or feisty, inappropriate and

sexual". I promise you we have played from sun up to

sun down and haven't even realized it. I love this

damn game. I'm not sure how I missed it but when I

look back up I see Edward standing over near one of

the windows. He's casually dressed in some jeans and

a white t-shirt and when he turns around I see that his

shirt reads "Sex with me is Priceless" and it adorns the

Master Card logo. He's my spirit animal I giggle to

myself before quickly looking around to see who's

looking.

"Hey stranger, you come here often" I say as I walk up

behind him and tap him on the shoulder. When he

turns to me he smiles with every muscle in his face

like I was the missing puzzle piece that he'd been

looking for. "Hi gorgeous, how have you been" he

said. "Great, but you would have known that had you

reached out to me or even responded to my text today" I replied sarcastically. He smirked and looked down at his shoes to avoid eye contact then looked up shyly. "I take it you didn't get any of my messages, catered lunches or flowers, or did they get lost in the field of flowers that you receive daily. Not to mention the fact that I've been without a phone for about a week now" he replied just as sarcastically as he showed me a crushed iPhone. "I figured that I was just another victim to another beautiful face" he added. It was getting louder and louder by the minute so I suggested that we go someplace quieter and led him up to the rooftop deck. Tonight's skyline proved that you don't have to have a passport to be transported to another place. You can find your paradise within the person you're with or even within yourself. Palm trees and white sand beaches are nice and should be visited as often as life allows but don't let it be the main ingredient in happiness.

We stand in silence for what seems like forever before we both start to speak at the same time. "I apologize, you go first" I say. "No, ladies first, I insist" he interrupted. "Well, thank you. I'm not one to bite my tongue or let things go unsaid. I don't believe in regrets especially if you were presented the opportunity to control your destiny. Although from the outside looking in, I might be completely out of your lea-" I stop before I proceed. "Wait, I thought that you said your phone was broken" I said. "That is correct" he replied. "So, how did you know about tonight? I text that information to you this morning" I interrogated. "Justin told me this morning when he picked me up from the airport. He told me that he was coming tonight with his girlfriend and suggested that I come too if I wasn't too tired. Tired or not, I was coming" he said in a way that I should have already known. "His girlfriend, who's his girlfriend, do I know her" I asked bewildered. "You're kidding me right now, right" he asked confused. "Ashlyn and Justin have been talking for quite some time now. I think they are kind of a thing. He sort of reminds me of myself at his age. Full of life and ideas. The young man has promise I'll tell you that much" he finished. "How do you know so much about his personal life? You guys only met that once when we went to dinner" I said. "What gives you that idea? He's been my driver for a few years now" he said as he smiled. At this point I am completely confused and apparently he sees it as well. "Erica, I think we need to take a few steps back before we go any further" he added. "Before you asked about how I found out you were saying something; it almost sounded like an omission to something. You were saying that you were completely out of something, what was that" he added. "I was saying that from the outside looking in that it might appear that I am completely out of your league" I began as Edward started to laugh uncontrollably. "What am I missing Edward, what is so funny" I say as he tried unsuccessfully to control himself. "Okay, let me get this right, you have made the decision to lower your standards and give little old me a chance" he said wiping tears from his eyes. "Yes, but I'm starting to have second thoughts" I replied starting to get annoyed. "Wait, before you get upset. May I please ask why you think that I am, for lack of a better word, struggling" he asked. "I'm not judging you in any way, I have much respect for anyone working and making an honest living" I answered.

"And, what is it that you believe that I do, if you don't mind me asking" he interrupted. "You're a barista, right. I saw you when you were filling out the application the first day we met" I replied.

Edward walked away over near the edge of the building. "I'm perfectly content with that just so you know" I interjected so that he wouldn't feel embarrassed. "Well Erica, first and foremost I have to tell you how much of a relief it is that you don't hold any negative judgements toward someone living a modest lifestyle and then to go even further to lower your standards to give me a chance. I swear, you have made my entire evening" he said as he became lost in my eyes. "But I have something to confess before we go any further" he said. "This has to be the story of my life. What, are you he married, gay or both? I'll do many things but I won't be your, on the other side of the fence girl" I replied angrily. He stared deeply into

my eyes and said, "There seems to be a huge

misunderstanding. I'm not a barista, well, not unless I

need to be. When you saw me that morning, I was

having a business meeting with my manager and

confirming the new job applications for new hires. I'm

the owner of "Cup of Joe" and it's actually a franchise

with thirty locations all together. Justin has been my

driver for years and I am CEO of several other

companies. I make it my business to visit all of my

locations especially when we decide to add new

avenues of making money, like the comedy night or

speed dating" as he continues I can feel a shade of

embarrassment cover my face that would probably be

there for the next one hundred years. I am still quiet

because it's hard to talk when your foot is in your

mouth. "To be perfectly honest, this match-up was

initiated by your friends and family and co-workers. I met Ashlyn a while back at the coffee shop and she was the first to actually mention you and suggested that we meet but suggested that I be completely prepared before we finally meet. From that moment I had a crash course in ERICA 101. I met with your mom **@eventsbyvilinda**, sister, all of your friends, Tabitha, Sheric, Dawn, Charmone, Denise...let's see, Drea, Air'Reon **@_symone15**, Tasha **@jusnatasha**, Angel , Vestina **@princessvestina**, Shakira **@genkieshakira**; actually all of the Social Butterflies had a part in this. Your family and friends truly love you, they just thought that you could use a hand. But never in a million years did I think that you were under the impression that I was just some guy who worked in a coffee shop. Everyone told me that you had a set of standards that you required a person to meet and there's nothing wrong with that at all, because so do

I" he added. "But it is very refreshing to know that you

learned something about yourself. That in all honesty

has probably made you an even better "you" and an

even greater catch, so I'm confident to say that I'm

the one winning here" he said in closing. "I feel so

unbelievably stupid right now because it's so unlike

me to jump to conclusions. I have to apologize for

assuming when I should have just asked. But after it

didn't matter there really wasn't any point in bringing

it up because by then I was ready to increase my

coffee intake until I had you" I said. Before I could

finish he grabbed me and kissed me sending electricity

running through every part of my body. I'm ready to

walk back in there and put everyone out like "Martin"

before we are interrupted by someone clearing their

throat. When we look over we see my clique both

family and friends. The moment is so magical and it seems like time is standing still just for us. The silence is broken when Melanie interrupts by saying "Sometimes the coach needs the team to win the game, but the rest is up to you". She's right, prior to this my motto was "Hi I heard you were a player, I'm the coach" but now that doesn't even really mean anything anymore. Sometimes the teacher becomes the student and all I can say about that is...Lesson Learned!

"School's Out"

Editor's Note

First and foremost, THANK YOU for your support and I look forward to bringing you many more books after this. Please understand that the story in this book is fictitious and the names used do not depict any specific person, place or thing. If I used your name or likeness in this or any other creative venture it is truly done out of LOVE and RESPECT!

Although I'm sure you understand that I couldn't possibly highlight EVERY person I know; please know that you are loved and appreciated...and you might be coming soon to a book or movie near you!

"BE ON THE LOOKOUT"

"Words That Fit"
The new card game created designed to mirror the personalities of those playing it. One of the only games that can go from the "Classroom to the Bedroom".

"You've Got Love"
The new relationship kit for ALL levels of relationships, both intimate and family.

"The Perfect Shoe"
A new interchangeable women's shoe that brings both high fashion and unique styles at an affordable price.

Made in the USA
Columbia, SC
12 October 2020

22678956R00176